Spirit Chamber

Books by Jay Hosler and Peggy Harrison

Norm and Burny: The Black Square

The Girl with the Gold Coin: Norm and Burny Book Two

Rockslide: Journals from the Age of Copper

Spirit Chamber

Book Two of the *Benchland* series

Five thousand years ago—late in the Age of Copper—two desperate couples found winter refuge in a cave. Exploring miles of subterranean passages, they discovered an exit onto the Benchland, a three-mile-long shelf of fertile ground, an isolated and beautiful place of wildflower, forest, and stream, set high on the steep wall of a river canyon and completely inaccessible to roving raiders, the scourge of that time in Europe. With ample game, year-round water, and firewood, the Benchland became home to the four founders and generations of their descendants.

The *Benchland* series is based on paintings the original settlers left on the walls of the cave—a pictorial diary of the colony, now an archaeological and historic treasure.

Spirit Chamber recounts events in the lives of the colony's second and third generations and tells of the discovery of the cave and its paintings by modern scientists who find, deep within the cave, a mysterious and spectacular place of power that binds them to the original settlers—the spiritual heart of the Benchland colony . . . the Spirit Chamber.

The sequel to *Rockslide*

Benchland Book Two

SPIRIT CHAMBER
Tales from the Benchland

Jay Hosler and Peggy Harrison

Spirit Chamber is a work of fiction. Its characters, events, and places are either the product of the authors' imagination or are used fictionally. Any resemblance to actual events or places, or to persons living or dead, is entirely coincidental.

This book contains excerpts from *Ring of Fire*, by Jay Hosler and Peggy Harrison. The excerpts have been set for this edition only and may not reflect the content of the published edition.

Cover photograph used with permission of Jay Hosler

Printed in the United States of America

ISBN-13: 978-0692504635
ISBN-10: 069250463X

Published by Benchland Publishing
admin@benchlandpubs.com

First edition
Revised September 2016

For

Joyce Gibson Roach

Historian, author, mentor, friend

Contents

PART ONE

LIGHT FROM THE STREAM

Light from the Stream is set nineteen years after *Rockslide*. It is narrated by Ana, daughter of Zoan and Quitana.

All the ancient characters of *Spirit Chamber* are listed in **Glossary of Names** at the end of the book.

1

"MOTHER! TRAVELERS!"

I am the first to see them, far below me—four people walking on the river road at midday. They are the first travelers this year, which is well along. Already the days are much shorter, and the trees are turning.

Mother and Aunt Inge come to the cliff, accompanied by the dog, who is outraged that people she doesn't know would dare venture into her territory. Her barking catches the attention of the travelers, and they stop, all looking up. Aunt Inge raises her arms, and one of the men below returns the greeting.

"Inge, is it anyone we know?" Mother strains to see, but as always she remains some distance from the cliff edge, and the road below is out of her sight.

"Three men and a woman," Aunt Inge says. "They don't appear to have weapons." She runs to the shelters for her bow and arrows and climbs down to the halfway ledge with bow and quiver slung over her shoulder. She has never liked to greet strangers unarmed.

Aunt Inge is still the fastest climber, even faster than Geyr, who is taller and stronger and much younger. The cliff face is almost vertical, and as she lets herself down the rope, jumping from rock to rock, you would think she was sixteen, not over thirty. She shows me how strong you can be when you're older. Aunt Inge loves climbing and walking at the very edge of the cliff. That's the way I want to be when I'm her age.

From the ledge she scrambles down to the deserted village beside the river, where she talks to the travelers for a long time. Mother, seedling plants in hand, returns to her work in the garden.

When Aunt Inge returns, one of the group climbs with her, a young man. I hear the two laugh together as they make the difficult climb, and when they reach the clifftop he is clearly delighted with the view. Aunt Inge leads him up to me. "Ana, this is Olaf. His parents and his uncle will wait in the village. We'll help them up to the bench."

Olaf smiles at me. "You have this view every day! Birds would envy it. You can see all the way to the sea!" He appears to be about fifteen, the first visitor ever who is a boy close to my age. The boys I know are the ones I grew up with. Geyr is always with Angela, my older sister, and pays no attention to me. In any case, he is nothing like me. His little brother Brandr is six, and the only other boys in my life are my brothers Druian and Aramel, and Aunt Inge's boys Leif and Kyle, who are too young for me. Soon I will be a grown woman, and ever since I was small I have wondered how I would find a husband in a place with no boys. Aunt Inge smiles and says that problem will solve itself someday. I know Olaf is only a temporary visitor, but it's a nice surprise to meet a boy my age.

Even though I already knew he was coming.

BEFORE OLAF'S VISIT, the most exciting time for me was five years ago, when I was eight. I went with Mother, Father, Angela, and Druian to the village of Northpoint, where Mother and Father grew up, to meet my grandparents. The boat trip took almost a month, and I loved every moment. First we had to walk for days to Rivermouth, the fishing village where the river empties into the sea. That walk scared me, because I kept thinking about bears, like the one that hurt Father before I was born. That bear was huge—we still have the skin—and the possibility of being attacked by a bear occurred to me every day of the walk to Rivermouth.

Tears flowed when we arrived in Northpoint. Both my grandfathers had died since Mother and Father last saw them twelve years before. Angela was a baby on that earlier trip and didn't remember it, but our grandmothers remembered her and cried, and they were sweet to me. Mother and Father were sad about their fathers, but they enjoyed seeing both my grandmothers and all three of my aunts, with their families. We stayed much longer than we had planned. We lived in the house where Mother grew up, which was beautiful, and I could look out and see the ocean. Northpoint is a fishing village, far south of the Benchland and much warmer. I saw boats every day, and we often ate fish.

My grandmothers always introduced me as Ana, Quitana's younger girl. They told me about Mother and Father when they were little, and how Father and Uncle Sigurd saved the village from the raiders, a story I've heard all my life, along with the story of the bear.

Really. Saved them from vicious raiders, in a big battle. And Mother and Aunt Inge and Grandmother too, all heroes. *My* mother.

I loved Northpoint, which had many children my age. I wanted to live there with my grandmothers, but Mother and Father said no—their mothers were too old to take care of an eight-year-old. So I came back, but I told myself I didn't want to live my entire life and raise my children in a place that had no ocean, or boats, or fish to eat.

What a lucky thing for me that I came back.

"WE SAW A BEAR yesterday. It looked at us but went away." Olaf is sitting with me on the old bearskin, which shows its age. The men are busy helping Olaf's family up to the bench.

"They're not as dangerous this late in the year." I feel foolish telling Olaf anything about bears. He undoubtedly knows all about them. He has blond hair and blue eyes, like Aunt Inge and her family, but he is taller. He has a friendly smile. Star is with us, and Olaf scratches her ears while we talk, which surprises me. She is half wolf and has always been shy around visitors.

"Where do you live in the winter? Surely not in these shelters."

"In the cave. I'll show you." We walk beside the stream into the cavern that shades the cave entrance, and he looks up in astonishment at the high ceiling. At the rear of the cavern, we duck through the entrance into the cave. Star prefers the outdoors and doesn't join us.

Once our eyes adjust to the dim light, we can see the entire length of our sleeping chamber—the stream running through it, our supplies stored against one wall, and our two cooking areas. The cave feels chilly after the warmth of the fall afternoon. "It's like this year round," I tell him, "never colder. Even when the stream outside is covered with ice."

We walk all the way to the back wall, and Olaf peers up the tunnel that leads to the spirit chamber. "How far back does the cave go?"

I hadn't intended to take him to the spirit chamber, but I can see he wants to go. "The tunnel leads into a completely dark room. We'll need torches."

I pick up two torches from the stack beside the tunnel, and the bag with fire tools and tinder. Then we crawl up the sloping tunnel.

What would it be like to see the spirit chamber for the first time? I grew up with it, and to me it is beautiful beyond my ability to tell. It is huge like the sleeping chamber, but otherwise very different. The spirit chamber is totally dark, but spectacular by torchlight. The stream curves through tall pillars of sparkling rock, hundreds of them, receding into the far distance, and the pool at the near end is deep and still and clear. The spirit chamber looks magical, and it feels like a living thing, aware, watching over me, protecting me.

The spirit chamber gives me dreams. That's how I knew Olaf would come.

AUNT INGE TOLD ME that as a baby I cried all the time, except in the spirit chamber. Yrsa told them I must visit there often. She was Geyr's grandmother; he remembers her from when he was small. I was born there, at midwinter. Most of us children were born there, all except Geyr. I know the spirit chamber by heart—every pillar and passageway. And I know the spirit, as much as you can know anything so big, and it knows everything about me—all my secrets.

The passage to the spirit chamber slopes steadily upward and comes out in the dark, high above the stream, on a hillside of jumbled rock. I usually climb down in the dark. I plan to light a torch for Olaf, but first we sit on a big rock near the top to wait for our eyes to adjust.

"It feels like something is watching us," he says. After a pause, he adds, "I love the sound of the stream. This place is alive. It knows we're here. I can feel it."

All my life I've been trying to explain that to the other children, but they simply don't understand. Nobody does except Mother and Aunt Inge. I thought the spirit was for women. Until Olaf.

I GREW UP loving my family, all of them, especially Mother and Aunt Inge, healers who share the spirit chamber with me. But I have always been the sort of child who needs time alone and does what she pleases. I went hunting with Father and Uncle Sigurd from the cave's west entrance. Getting there means climbing a steep scary rock wall, and I loved it. When I was ten I climbed that wall alone, and from the west entrance I hiked to the top of the mountain, where I saw the Benchland from above. Nobody else has done that, and I'm still proud of it, even though I agreed with Father afterward that I should not have gone alone. And over the years, dragging Druian with me at Father's insistence, I have explored every last passage in our vast cave.

All my life I have been drawn to the spirit chamber. I have seen it in dreams since I was tiny, and I have been there every day since I was old enough to go alone. I often frightened everyone by going to the spirit chamber without a torch. I don't need light. The spirit chamber has its own kind of light—I find my way by the sound of the water. Even Mother and Aunt Inge need torches.

When I light the torch, Olaf surprises me. He catches his breath, and his eyes are wide. "It looks exactly the way it sounds." He picks his way down the boulders to the pool. I follow, and we sit beside the stream, facing each other. Olaf notices the small hearth we use for ceremonies.

"We have fires here sometimes. I was born in this room."

"The water flows into the stream outside," he says, "and over the cliff into the river, and into the sea. I can feel it going there. Listen. You can hear it. It's all connected."

I close my eyes to listen. How have I not heard all this before?

We sit for a long time, hearing the stream going to the light and the sea. I always feel the spirit in this chamber, but now I feel Olaf's presence as well. I open my eyes to find him looking at me, and as we gaze at each other my world falls away until nothing remains but Olaf, the spirit, and the sound of the stream.

Am I still breathing? My heart pounds, out of control.

The torch burns out, but the spirit has forged a link between us that darkness cannot break. I have become part of something new.

THE DAY IS NEARLY OVER when Olaf and I emerge. The evening is chilly, and everyone is gathered around a fire. Mother is relieved to see us but cross with me. She knew where we were, because she saw I had taken the fire tools. She told Olaf's parents we were in the cave and would be safe. She wisely didn't say we had taken only two torches and were surely in the dark, or that I went often into the totally dark cave with no torches at all.

Mother presents me to Olaf's parents, Andor and Folke, and Andor's brother, Ingvar. After Folke presents Olaf, I lead him to the other fire, where Angela and Geyr are feeding the children, and introduce him. That's when I see how tall he is—as tall as Geyr.

When we return to the adults, Father is talking with Ingvar, a fisherman. He was only fourteen when he fought under Uncle Sigurd in the famous battle. He is astonished to find himself in the company of its heroes.

"You're far from home, Ingvar."

"Our father left Andor and me two fishing boats. I came north to tell him. From Rivermouth, I walked north a halfmonth. I passed by here nearly a month ago and had no idea you were up here."

Olaf sits with his mother, across the fire from me. Like Geyr, he has blue eyes and light blond hair, but there the resemblance ends. I have seen Geyr almost every day of my life, but after one visit to the spirit chamber I know Olaf better, and when he looks at me this evening it feels as if we share a secret.

Aunt Inge catches one of those looks and understands everything. "We went to the pool," I tell her. "He sensed the spirit. I had already taken him there, in a dream."

Aunt Inge knows the spirit chamber better than anyone except me. "Ana," she says quietly, "dreams are important, but you must make decisions about your life in your waking mind."

"I could feel his presence even in the dark. The feeling came from the spirit. Our thoughts joined. He heard the water going to the sea." I know Aunt Inge understands. I also happen to know that she was my age when she and Uncle Sigurd were married, so she isn't likely to tell me I am too young.

"I'M HAPPY to move south," Olaf's father says. "I've had enough of bitter weather."

Father raises his eyebrows. "It's late in the year for a long voyage."

"Ingvar is a master seaman. He knows how to deal with bad weather."

I barely hear. I am thinking of my discussion with Aunt Inge, and I never take my eyes off Olaf. I don't know what will happen, but the spirit would never betray me.

The guests sleep in Angela and Geyr's shelter, near the garden, while Angela and Geyr camp near the edge of the cliff. The evening is beautiful, with a perfect full moon, and as I lie on my sleeping pallet I can feel Olaf's presence, as if we were still sitting facing each other in the spirit chamber. I can think of nothing else.

I WAKE IN THE MORNING full of happiness. That lasts only until I join the group around the fire, because Olaf and his family are preparing to depart, as if nothing had changed.

The reality of their departure falls on me like a deadly illness. I have trouble breathing and can't speak. Around me, everything seems normal. The adults talk with each other as usual. For me, the world has stopped.

At first I don't dare look at Olaf, for fear of bursting into tears. Then we exchange a glance of desperation. We walk to the edge of the cliff, but no words come. After the spirit chamber, we hardly talked; we didn't need to. Now, with the memory of that time swirling around us, I realize that I know almost nothing about Olaf. I don't know what kind of man he is. Would he be a good husband and father? Would he fit into our group? Does he even feel the way I do?

I can't look at him. He would see my anguish.

"Ana—" he begins, but doesn't finish. Finally he says, "I could hunt for our food," and in that moment our lives are set.

WHEN WE REJOIN THE GROUP, Olaf's father snaps, "Get your pack. We've been waiting for you."

"I'd like to stay longer." Olaf speaks quietly. "Ana and I don't wish to part yet."

I expect shock and anger from Mother, but Aunt Inge must have warned her when we walked away. When I am an adult I hope I will have some of Aunt Inge's understanding and wisdom.

The shock comes from Olaf's father. "This once, you'll do as you're told." He is instantly in a fury—red face, bulging neck veins—and he advances menacingly on Olaf. I feel a jolt of fear.

Olaf does nothing to defend himself. His mother steps in front of him, and Olaf's father slaps her brutally to the ground. Her bloody face horrifies me, and Olaf turns to kneel beside her. Olaf's father turns angrily on him, but Uncle Sigurd stops the fight by stepping forward and lifting Olaf's father off the ground from behind. "Your wife and son are guests and under our protection. I will not let you harm them." Uncle Sigurd is over forty but still a powerful man, and Olaf's father cannot free himself. When he stops struggling, Uncle Sigurd sets him down.

Olaf's father whips around, his face contorted with rage. A short dagger appears in his hand.

"Andor, NO!" Olaf's uncle seizes his brother's arm and wrenches the knife away. Star rushes into the fray, and her barking makes a bad situation worse. Olaf's mother is on her feet, crying in Olaf's arms.

"You must leave," Uncle Sigurd says. Star stands at his side, bristling and growling.

"Oh, yes, we'll leave." Olaf's father gestures angrily to his wife and son, but she shakes her head, and Olaf draws her to the other side of the fire, safely beyond reach. I fear this will bring another attack, but Olaf's father sees Uncle Sigurd watching him and thinks better of it. "Stay, then, and be forever cursed."

At the edge of the cliff he glares back at Uncle Sigurd. "You will regret this." Then, his hand on the rope, he turns to me, and his face is one of pure hatred. "*You*—you put him under a spell. You hexed him. We know how to deal with people like you."

We all stand in stunned silence as he starts down the rope. He is no climber, and his clumsiness only makes him angrier. His brother is obviously embarrassed. He spreads his hands and apologizes. Then he too goes to the rope and starts down the cliff.

I feel as if I have been slapped in the face—my cheeks burn, and my heart races. Olaf's father doesn't even know me. Why does his anger wound me so?

Beside the river, Olaf's uncle grabs his brother's arm and swings him around, and the two argue heatedly. We can barely hear them, and we cannot understand their words. They start down the river road, still arguing, and pass out of sight before the sun reaches the village.

OUR BENCHLAND is a shelf halfway up a sheer mountainside—a natural fortress with a dizzying drop to the river on the east and a mountain wall on the west. Except for scaling the cliff, the only way to reach the bench is by coming through the cave, as my parents and Uncle Sigurd and Aunt Inge did originally. They had taken winter refuge in the cave near the west entrance, which is far from here—on the other side of the mountain. Mother and Father found the bench while they were exploring the cave. When the four of them saw that the bench had security and year-round water, they moved their camp. The route through the cave is long and confusing, with its own dangerous climbing. It requires torches, because the entire route lies in total darkness. I know exactly when the elders first came to the bench, because Mother was pregnant with Angela, who is eighteen, and in all those years, no one else has discovered the bench through the cave.

We live near the south end of the bench, where it is narrow. It extends some distance north of the cave. It is wider there but still confined between the cliff edge on the east and the high mountain on the west. The view eastward is beautiful, over diminishing hills to the distant seashore. Deer gather at a large spring-fed pool not far from here. The bench has dense forests, and the entire area is a flower garden in summer, with birds and butterflies.

The climb from the river to the bench is difficult even with the help of a rope. Father was the first to climb it. The ropes were made of braided hide then, but by the time I was a little girl, we had hempen rope, which is stronger and lighter than hide. We grow our own hemp. When Fedr was young, one of his jobs was digging up wild hemp plants from the riverside and planting them beside the spring in the sun, where they thrived. Fedr tends them still. Twisting hemp fibers into thread is a good job for children, and Fedr makes ropes from the thread. His hands are gnarled from years of twisting hemp into the strong ropes we use for climbing and hauling. When we have visitors, we haul them up to the bench in hide harnesses with two ropes. Olaf is one of the few visitors to climb the rope without assistance.

I tell this to dispel any idea that Olaf's father might return and attack us. Deer find their way down to the bench from the mountaintop, along scanty rock ledges only they know, but for people and bears the bench might as well be on the moon.

MY ANGER and embarrassment don't last long after Olaf's father leaves, but Folke is speechless with humiliation, and she is in pain besides. She and Olaf huddle together, and I see how much they look alike, with the same blond hair and blue eyes. She looks small beside him, too young to have a son his age. Mother draws her to the fire, where they talk as Folke weeps and holds a wet hide to her bloody face. Aunt Inge pours tea and joins the conversation. Uncle Sigurd talks quietly to Father and Fedr. He seemed calm when he lifted Olaf's father, but now his anger is plain.

Olaf stands by himself. He looks at me, but I see no secret smiles. We walk away from the group again, but without talking, and I think about what has happened. My life has turned upside down. I discovered that Olaf and I share something profound and then learned he was about to leave. Now everything has changed again because he will stay. Joy, horror, and now relief—but mixed with anxiety, because he and his mother are in pain.

What kind of man would attack his wife and son?

"I hate him." Olaf is close to tears and trembles with anger as his words rush out. "I've wished for years that Mother and I could get away from him. He has hurt us both, again and again. I've been afraid of him as long as

I can remember, afraid he would kill us. You saw what he's like. My grandparents and our neighbors all disliked him, because they knew he beat her. That's why he was glad to leave the village. Mother was only fifteen—my age—when I was born. I think he resented her and never wanted me. I hope a bear kills him. At least I hope I never see him again."

Olaf falls silent. I feel his anger and the hot ashes of his fear, but nothing of the deep connection we shared yesterday. I lead him into the cave. His mother will deal with her fear and shock in her own way, with help from Mother and Aunt Inge. For Olaf, the best medicine is time with me in the spirit chamber. It seems selfish, but that fills me with fierce joy.

I light a torch and lead Olaf to my private spot. I have a feeling of oneness with the spirit there, and I have never before shared my spot with anyone. When I was small, I thought it was mine alone. In time I felt the lingering presence of others who found it before me—Aunt Inge and her teacher Yrsa, at least.

I need that place now. It will calm me and perhaps give Olaf strength and courage.

"Sit here." I extinguish the torch and sit facing him—wordless, in darkness, surrounded by the sound of the stream. We do not touch, but I can feel that Olaf is rigid with tension. It seems a long time before his breathing slows.

The voice of the stream changes from moment to moment. Olaf hears it as the sound of the spirit, and now, as he relaxes, the sound grows. In a rush, I feel him emerge from his shell of isolation. He takes my hands between his—our first intimate touch—and we sit silently until the feeling of us together fully replaces the rage of the morning.

We lean forward until our foreheads meet, still without a word, and I lose track of time.

It is afternoon before we rejoin the others around the fire. Olaf's mother looks spent as she talks quietly to Mother and Aunt Inge. When we approach, she looks up and smiles at Olaf, but her eyes are full of sorrow.

Aunt Inge looks at me, and I see that she understands everything, as usual.

IN ALL MY LITTLE-GIRL YEARS of wondering how I would find a husband, it never occurred to me that the best man for me might come to the Benchland. I thought I would have to go to Mother's village. My notion of what I wanted grew out of the old stories Mother told me, tales of girls overcome by love for some perfect man— hero, hunter, lover. The stories were about many different girls, but I saw myself in each one. I didn't think I could settle for a love like Angela and Geyr's— they do love each other, despite their quarreling. Their marriage is a natural result of growing up together and a willingness to accept what was available. And despite the obvious affection between Mother and Father, I can't imagine they were ever overwhelmed by loving, which is what I want for myself.

I never before understood that I crave a deep union of spirit. I learned that by loving Olaf, who meets me as an equal and treats our bond with tenderness and respect. Together in the spirit chamber, where we have shared thoughts and feelings from the first visit, we see beyond the material world, stepping around the usual boundaries between people. How could I have known that was what I wanted?

FATHER AND UNCLE SIGURD leave early in the morning for a hunting trip of several days. They would have left yesterday but for the guests. Father deeply enjoys their traditional late autumn trip. When I was small, he would take me onto his lap afterward and tell me what he had seen, mixing in outlandish adventures that definitely never occurred, told with his eyes twinkling. Even then, I didn't believe he actually met a flying bear. His joy in hunting was clear, though, and I loved those times with him.

Often Fedr goes along, or Geyr or Druian. Aunt Inge goes sometimes, but she says she enjoyed hunting more when she was younger. Mother says she has made her last hunting trip, and Angela will never make her first. She and I see almost everything differently, and hunting is no exception. I was flattered when Father invited me to go two years ago and again last year, and I will remember those adventures forever. On this trip Father and Uncle Sigurd will be by themselves, which I secretly suspect they like most of all. They have hunted together for twenty years.

"Where are they *going*?" Olaf is surprised when they say goodbye—and then disappear into the cave. He expected them to climb down the cliff to the river.

He goes on before I have time to answer. "The cave must have another entrance! Not close to the river, or you'd be using it. It must be on the other side of the mountain."

He looks at me. "Show me." His eyes are alight.

No one knows our cave as I do. Seeing it all would require a month of trips. To me it is endlessly fascinating. When I found an upper entrance high above the bench, not far below the mountaintop, I took Father to see it. He loves the cave, but even he didn't share my excitement. No one ever has—until now.

Olaf's reaction delights me, but I am not surprised, knowing that we respond the same way to the spirit chamber.

I lead him into the sleeping chamber and then back to the far northwest corner, where I have drawn a map of the cave. He sees what it is immediately. "Look," he says, pointing, "we're standing right here."

"It's only a charred-stick sketch so far. Someday I'll paint it, now that it's finally complete. I spent two years drawing it."

He stands back and takes in the map, and his amazement is obvious. "The cave is *huge*. I want to see it all."

"I will show it to you. All of it. But that will take time, and work comes first." Olaf and I will help with the harvest, but this morning we will set up a sleeping site for him and his mother near the adults' hearth. Next spring we will build a new summer shelter; that wouldn't make sense this late in the year. Winter is hard on the shelters, and we have more than enough work now, taking in our fall crops—grain, hemp, beans, and squash.

At breakfast, Folke stares into the distance, perhaps struggling to understand what has happened. I can sympathize. The foundations of her life have collapsed. She's better off for escaping a vicious man, but now she's in an unknown situation.

I move to sit beside her. "Can I help?"

My question breaks her reverie. "It's kind of you to set up the sleeping area, Ana. You're already doing so much for me."

Folke smiles. Even in her misery, she obviously takes pleasure in the joy of my bond with Olaf.

"I LOVE HUNTING," Olaf says, "especially in the fall. I envy them, setting out on a long trip." We talk while we work, carrying rocks to make a private alcove for him and

Folke. We can't lift the biggest boulders and must work together to roll them into place.

"I love hunting too. Fall hunting trips with Father and Uncle Sigurd are wonderful."

"They took you along?"

"Last year and the year before. You and I can hunt on the bench. It has game, although not as much now. I'll show you the entire bench, and if we're lucky we could shoot a deer. Maybe Aunt Inge will come."

"I'll need arrows. I'll start making them today."

"Father can show you how to make glarestone points." Glarestone is a glossy black stone that can be chipped into the sharpest points and blades. It is rare and normally hard to find, but we are fortunate to have an entire hillside of it only a short distance up the river.

"I've seen him working with it. Learning to do that will take time. For now, I have three flint points. I need to make new shafts."

We place the last rock and go outside to rest in the sun. "Everyone seems to accept Mother and me," Olaf says. "I'm surprised by such a welcome. When did you last take in new people?"

"Before I was born. Fedr came when he was young. The day he arrived, he killed the bear. Geyr's mother and grandparents came about the same time."

We sit in silence. The trees behind Olaf are brilliant in their fall colors, and I see him within a magical aura of yellow and gold.

"So much has happened in such a short time," he says. "Two days ago I didn't know you existed, but I feel as if I've known you all my life."

"I saw you a month ago in a dream, but I had no hint of what would happen to us in the spirit chamber."

Mother and Aunt Inge appear on the path from the garden, carrying bundles of grain. They are laughing, but Folke, following them, looks downcast. Aunt Inge smiles when she sees us.

"That's why they accept me and my mother," Olaf says. "They understand that the spirit has put you and me together."

OLAF AND I go to the spirit chamber every day. It isn't long before Olaf can find his way by the sound of the stream as well as I, so we stop using torches. My private place—a large flat rock in the pool—becomes ours. We lie side by side there, not touching but completely connected, wrapped in the sound of the stream and the feeling of the spirit.

I sleep, and dream of Eydis, Aunt Inge's younger daughter.

Eydis has cut her arm and is frightened by the blood. Angela has taken her to the stream to bind the cut. Eydis adores Angela and loves the attention from her, but she continues to sob.

I am slow to realize that Olaf is trying to wake me. He is alarmed. "Eydis—"

"You saw her too?"

"Ana, I felt you there. I knew we were sharing the dream. And I knew we were seeing a real event."

Olaf and I stare at each other in wonder.

By the time we arrive at the shelters, Eydis's cut is bound up, and she cheerfully accepts comfort from Angela and Aunt Inge. Eventually Angela returns to work. Aunt Inge smiles at me and Olaf. "Ana, you look puzzled."

"We were in the spirit chamber and shared a dream of Eydis, with her arm cut. We saw that in a dream, both of us, as it was happening."

Aunt Inge hesitates. "Dreams of seeing are gifts of the spirit. I know them, and Yrsa did as well. Nothing that happens to you in the spirit chamber surprises me. You are closer to the spirit than any of us, because you've grown up with it. And sharing a dream with Olaf! Perhaps that is part of your connection to him."

After that Olaf and I take hides on our visits to the spirit chamber, and dreaming together becomes part of our lives.

WHEN FATHER AND UNCLE SIGURD aren't hunting, they spend most days at their work area, where they built a large rock oven for baking pots and heating redmetal, a hard lightweight shiny material that they shape with heat and hammers. Redmetal makes fine knife blades and arrowheads, but also ornaments; Mother wears a beautiful redmetal ring I have always admired.

The redmetal comes from a greenish rock dug from a hillside near the abandoned village on the river. Father and Uncle Sigurd melt the rock and pour it into molds. They have been doing this work for years, improving it over time. I remember a visitor—a master redmetal worker—who showed them how to make redmetal harder by adding a powdered stone to the melting pot, and told them where to find the stone.

The work fascinates Olaf, and I can understand. The roaring fire under the oven captivated me when I was small, even though the radiating heat felt dangerous as I cringed away from it, safe in Mother's arms. When the redmetal in the oven is hot enough, it pours like water, and I still feel fear as the men pour seething-hot redmetal into clay molds. The danger is real, because even the slightest contact with the hot materials leaves a terrible burn. Father and Uncle Sigurd both bear scars of old burns.

When they plunge the still-hot mold into cold water, the clay cracks away with a sound of its own, and I remember that too from my earliest years, along with a feeling of mystery, because the shining arrowheads and ornaments that emerge from the molds are so different from the green gravel they are made from.

The men do most of this work by themselves, although everyone participates in the hard work of hauling supplies up the cliff. Green gravel, the source of the redmetal, comes from the village. Firerock, the oven's fuel, comes from the ledge below.

Today Olaf and I are bringing firerock up to the work area. I climb down to the ledge and load hide bags; Olaf hauls each one up to the cliff edge and carries it to the work area, where he empties the bag onto the growing pile of firerock. He ties the empty bag to the rope and drops it down the cliff to me. By that time I have another bag loaded and ready to haul. I have done this work for years, with Geyr, but it is more enjoyable with Olaf, and in a day we bring up a prodigious pile of firerock. By sunset, we are both as black as the rock itself—faces, hands, arms, legs, clothes, all black.

CARVING IS AN IMPORTANT PART of Father and Uncle Sigurd's work, and both are masters. On my tenth birthday, they gave me a redmetal hunting dagger that I think is exquisite; Father finished the blade, and Uncle Sigurd carved the bone handle. They have always made our tools and weapons.

Olaf admires my dagger and wants to try a carving project of his own. He already has some experience—he makes excellent arrows. He finds Uncle Sigurd putting the finishing touches on a wooden axe handle, using a knife with a glarestone blade.

"I would like to learn to make tool handles. I have my own carving knife but use it only for arrows."

"I've seen your arrows, Olaf. They show care and craftsmanship. You should begin by making a carving knife with a blade of glarestone."

"I hope to begin working with glarestone this winter. For now, this is the only knife I have." He hands his knife to Uncle Sigurd, who examines it closely.

"It needs to be sharper." Uncle Sigurd hands Olaf a stubby piece of wood as thick as a thumb, but longer, with a bit of antler protruding from the end. "The antler tip is hard enough to sharpen your flint blade." He lays the knife blade on a flat rock and shows Olaf how to stroke it repeatedly with the sharpener, always in the same direction.

As Olaf industriously sharpens his knife, Uncle Sigurd finds a piece of hardwood the size of a wrist. "This is good for carving practice. It has a curving grain."

"What should I make?"

"Whatever you please. It's a learning project. Bring it to me when you're finished, and we'll talk about it. Be patient. Carving takes time."

Olaf takes the task seriously, working on his carving a little at a time, repeatedly putting it down and returning to it. After ten days he has a figure of a sleeping child whose hair flows with the grain of the wood. Olaf polishes the piece until it is smooth and feels like stone. It is beautiful but unlike the other carvings here, and Olaf fears Uncle Sigurd may think it unacceptable.

Uncle Sigurd holds the figure in his hands, turning it and looking at it. Eventually he looks at Olaf. "Excellent. The child was there in the wood, and you revealed it. When you are older you could be a master carver." He goes on to point out details that Olaf might have finished differently.

Olaf is relieved and grateful, and I see how happy he is that our group accepts him.

OLAF AND FOLKE have been with us only a halfmonth when the weather turns cold, ending our summer in the outdoor shelters. Bitter winds sweep the bench. Ice forms overnight in the still pools, and mornings are miserably cold, especially for the small children. Angela, who is pregnant and sick, is even more impatient than usual with Geyr and all of us.

Angela's pregnancy reminds me of the saddest time of my life, when Fedr's wife, Heidl, died in childbirth. I was nine and shaken to the core by such an awful example of a danger I too will someday face. I feared for Fedr too, because in his grief he didn't eat, and I saw he could die as well. I retreated to the spirit chamber for reassurance, but weeks passed before I felt whole again.

MOVING INSIDE for winter takes days. Father and Uncle Sigurd move their work area to a smaller oven under the cavern roof, still cold but never snow-covered. All the men help move tools and supplies. The rest of us empty the outdoor shelters, bring everything inside the cave, and set up sleeping areas near the two hearths. When I was small we had only a single cooking fire, but we soon became too many for that, and the confusion made everyone short-tempered, even Mother and Aunt Inge. Two hearths helped—one just for the children, with an adult supervising. After Geyr and Angela were married, they took over the children's hearth and slept near that fire.

We are now nineteen, the biggest our village has ever been. This winter Olaf and Folke will sleep near the adults' hearth. I am flattered and moved when Aunt Inge invites Olaf and me to join the adults for meals, and after we are married to sleep near the adults.

Angela tartly suggests that Olaf and I should take our turn at tending the children. "Of course," Mother says quickly, "as soon as Ana is the oldest daughter." She points out that before long, Angela will add her own baby to our growing crowd of little ones. I will hear more from Angela about the sleeping arrangements. She is a good daughter and a good sister, and I love her, but we have argued about everything for my entire life.

Star has always slept with the children, and she takes seriously her task of keeping them from wandering, a job she learned from her mother, Lyna, who kept me safe when I was small. Lyna was a half-dead puppy when Mother rescued her, but she grew up to be huge. She was black like Star. She lived almost fifteen years. I was seven when she died, and I cried for days. Star is every bit her equal, and even bigger. Star's father was an enormous tawny wolf who found his way down the deer trail onto the bench. I saw him once. He didn't stay, which was good for him—the men would have killed him if they could. Star was born when I was six. She is loving, gentle and intelligent, with tawny streaks and wolflike yellow eyes. She has never liked living in the cave, but reluctantly moves inside for the winter. I have always loved her fiercely, and sleeping without her will feel strange when I move away from the children's hearth.

IN THE SPIRIT CHAMBER, Olaf and I share a dream.

> The two of us are walking to Rivermouth because something has happened to the boat. We arrive late at night. The last quarter moon has risen. At first the boatyard seems to be as I remember it from six years ago, but then I see a pillar of smoke. I fear it comes from our boat. We run to where the boat is stored. The smoke is dissipating, but the boat is only charred timbers. I see a man running away. He knows we have seen him, and turns to glare threateningly at us. Olaf's father! I am frightened and angry.

We wake upset, knowing the boat is gone. Olaf's old anger boils over, and we remain in the spirit chamber until he is calm enough to bring our news to Father and Uncle Sigurd.

We find them near the adults' hearth, talking with Aunt Inge. Everyone else is at the other hearth, helping with the children.

"Ana, what is it?" Aunt Inge instantly sees that I am troubled.

"Olaf's father has burned our boat."

We immediately have the attention of Father and Uncle Sigurd. Father asks, "You dreamed this? You think it's happening right now?"

"We both saw it, in a shared dream. Olaf's father must have burned the boat as soon as he reached Rivermouth. When he was here, the moon was full. In the dream, it was a few days beyond full."

A long silence follows.

Uncle Sigurd speaks first. "He and his brother must be far south of here by now. The winter was nearly upon them. They would not have stayed long in Rivermouth."

Mother arrives from the children's hearth. "What happened?"

Father answers her. "Ana and Olaf dreamed of Olaf's father burning our boat."

Mother turns to me. "Ana, the little girls are more than Angela can manage tonight. Would you and Olaf help her, please? The four of us will discuss what to do."

I see we aren't yet full adults. The discussion upsets Olaf, though, and taking him away from it helps soothe my injured pride.

WHEN OLAF AND I rejoin the adults at the end of the evening, Father and Uncle Sigurd are preparing for a trip to Rivermouth. "If the boat is gone, we must arrange for a new one," Father says, "because we will need to make another trip home."

Uncle Sigurd paces, as he does when he is agitated. "Olaf's father will be more and more dangerous until we confront him. We should sail south in early spring, as soon as weather permits."

"I'd like to join you on this trip to Rivermouth," Fedr says. I know Olaf feels the same way.

Uncle Sigurd puts his hand on Fedr's shoulder. "You and Olaf will be a big help here." To Olaf, he says, "Your father won't be in Rivermouth, of course. He's long gone. We'll need you on the trip south, in the spring."

I understand Father and Uncle Sigurd. They want the fastest possible trip, which means by themselves. They have made that trip many times in summer; it takes at least three days in each direction. They hope to return before the first big snow, but the weather is threatening, and they will take snowfeet, along with weapons, food, and trade goods.

They depart before dawn. As they leave, I wonder how much longer they will be able to continue as our leaders, and what we will do afterward. Father is nearly forty, Uncle Sigurd still older. Younger men will take their places—Geyr, Olaf, and others—but today I acutely appreciate the importance of elders to a village. Their experience and wisdom require years to develop. The loss of an elder is a heavy blow.

Later, in the spirit chamber, I am thinking again of Father's and Uncle Sigurd's roles in our lives, when Olaf quietly says, "I'll do my best, but I will never be able to replace them. This group has succeeded because of the strength and wisdom of your elders." He lapses into silence, obviously feeling the weight of his responsibility to us.

WHEN FATHER AND UNCLE SIGURD RETURN, we are well established in the cave. Star's furious barking at the cliff edge alerts Aunt Inge, who sees the men approaching from the south and is down the rope and laughing in Uncle Sigurd's arms before they reach the village. A cold dreary rain is falling, and both men are wet through, but cheerful.

They found Karl still in charge of his boatyard, although he is too old to do the work. He remembers Olaf's father, who asked him about us and our boat. Karl wasn't suspicious, because he knows Olaf's uncle. Not long after the two brothers departed, Karl realized our boat was afire. He was horrified but wasn't able to save the boat.

I feel a deep personal loss. That boat carried me to Northpoint when I was eight, and I loved the trip. I have thought of the boat many times and have taken comfort that it was waiting for us in Rivermouth.

Father and Uncle Sigurd arrived at a bargain with Karl, who admired one of Father's spear points and accepted it as a token. He promised a boat by spring and showed them the hull, which is almost complete. It has been nearly twenty years since Karl sold them the original boat. The new one will be longer, faster, and more comfortable. It has a covered cabin and a new design, with two hempen sails. The trip south will be easier than the one I remember.

Olaf's anger returns whenever he thinks about next spring's journey south, because it reminds him anew of his father's treachery. The burning boat comes back to us many times in dreams, perhaps to ensure that Olaf doesn't forget about it, as if he could.

SNOW FALLS IN EARNEST a month and a half before midwinter, and we settle into our winter routine. The men make glarestone and redmetal arrow points for hunting and trade. The women sew and improve our living quarters, Folke working alongside Mother and Aunt Inge. She was ill used for so long by her husband that when she first arrived she was timid, almost afraid, speaking with a small voice and few words. Mother and Aunt Inge have been unfailingly warm and gentle with her, and how she has changed! Her eyes sparkle, and

Olaf says he hardly recognizes her as the fearful mother he knew.

We need Folke's skills. She is a good cook and a remarkable gardener. Her home village was south of Aunt Inge's. She knows the native plants on our Benchland as well as those Aunt Inge planted from seed years ago, and Folke brought seeds from her own garden as well. She is also a gifted storyteller with a wealth of tales and a talent for entertaining children. We have enough small children that this is a big help. She acts out her stories by the children's fire, making animal noises and using her hands to cast shadows. The enraptured children around her are often joined by amused adults.

As Folke recovers, her warm personality emerges. I have liked her from the beginning, and not only because I see her through Olaf's eyes. Her sweetness draws me to her, and we have become friends. We work together in the garden, hurrying to collect seeds and pick the last of the fruit to be dried for winter. She is a healer, which might explain Olaf's sensitivity to the spirit world. She and Aunt Inge spend many evenings talking about using plants and herbs in healing. Folke is one of us now, and I forget how recently she arrived. When she is alone, she must think about her life with Olaf's father, but she never speaks of it. She has never mentioned the confrontation with him here, and the night we discussed his burning the boat, she remained silent.

OLAF SPENDS MANY WINTER DAYS learning to work with glarestone. I often see him sitting with Father, their heads bent over their work. Father learned this craft from an old man in his home village and has taught Fedr, Geyr, and Druian. Olaf is his fourth student.

Olaf makes a set of tools like Father's—antler chippers of different shapes and sizes, set in wooden handles. The antler tips are hardened in the fire. Olaf tries each one at length, flaking sharp edges on test pieces. When he is ready, Father hands him a finished spear point to copy, one with a complex shape. Olaf works for days, with several false starts, and produces a fine point, but of a different design. He says it is like flint spear points he has made before, designed to be attached to a shaft quickly and securely. Father says it is good work, and valuable. Olaf is already at work on a carving knife, and his work area is always littered with shiny black bits of glarestone.

HUNTING TAKES MORE TIME during winter, when game is scarce and walking requires snowfeet. Years of hunting on the bench have thinned out the deer, and the men make extended hunting trips from the west entrance. Olaf loves hunting, and he is happy to join Father, Uncle Sigurd, and Fedr on their first trip of the winter. They return after four days with two fat deer. The men are overloaded, tired, and flushed with success.

Olaf is full of admiration for Father and Uncle Sigurd. "We saw no game until yesterday. Then we came across a deer herd grazing some distance away. Fedr and I hid in a grove while Uncle Sigurd and your father walked half the morning to get behind the deer and haze them our way. A big buck and a doe came almost to us. I shot the doe, but the buck spooked and bounded off. He was far away and moving fast when Uncle Sigurd and your father shot at him. We thought we had lost him, but we followed his trail and found him dead with both their arrows in him." Olaf pauses. "I've never known men who could shoot like that."

"You shoot well yourself, Olaf." Fedr has been listening. He too has always looked up to Father and Uncle Sigurd as the ultimate hunters. "You shot the first deer."

The fresh meat is welcome, and the successful hunt requires a feast. Folke and I help prepare the food, working with Mother and Aunt Inge. I see the two of them the way Olaf sees Father and Uncle Sigurd, as leaders whose skills I will never match. Some of my best childhood memories include Mother and Aunt Inge cooking together for our many feasts of celebration, laughing as they worked.

The feast begins with a prayer of thanks, sung by Aunt Inge, to express our gratitude to the deer. Our entire group is gathered, seated by the adults' hearth, with the children in front holding bone deer figures they see only at these feasts. Some of those carvings are older than I am. They were made from kills whose hide and meat are long gone. Now their role is to help the children understand our feelings about killing and eating fellow creatures.

In the midst of the glad celebration that evening, the moon rises out of the sea to the east, a few days beyond full. Moonlight reflects off the snow on the bench and shines directly into the cave entrance, briefly making our sleeping chamber extraordinary. I sit with Olaf, and as I look at him, I realize he is no longer the boy I met only two months ago. So much has happened since then—the shocking events of his arrival, our joining in spirit, and his becoming a working member of our group. Tonight he is a grown man, beautiful in the moonlight, tall and strong. He looks at me as he feels my eyes on him and smiles when he realizes what I want to say. Then, in front of everyone, I turn to Aunt Inge and ask her to join us in marriage at the midwinter full moon, less than a month away.

The group erupts into laughter and chatter, but no one is surprised that Olaf and I will marry. They welcome it, as they did Angela and Geyr's marriage, because they all know new unions make the group stronger—ours particularly, because Olaf brings us new blood.

Mother and Folke hug me tearfully. Father clasps Olaf's arms. Uncle Sigurd laughs and slaps Olaf on the back. Aunt Inge is jubilant. "I've been planning your wedding for two months, hoping you would catch on in time for the midwinter ceremony."

5

WHEN ANGELA AND GEYR WERE MARRIED a year and a half ago, I was surprised to find myself overwhelmed by emotion, full of tears of joy, for them and for us all. They had always been a couple. Why did their marriage seem so important? Part of it was Heidl, Geyr's mother, already gone two years that spring. The wedding ceremony, out on the bench in the full moon, is what finally brought Fedr back from two years of crushing grief. Fedr isn't Geyr's father, but loves him as his own; he raised him from infancy alongside his and Heidl's three younger children. Their two little girls sparkled around Angela and Geyr, laughing and singing, both looking like Heidl, especially Dota, the older of the two. I had never seen such energy from two-year-old Svala, who has a bad limp. We had all suffered when Heidl died, and that wedding celebration was like a rebirth for our community. I remember Aunt Inge, after speaking the ceremony and the prayers, laughing and crying at the same time, and when she and Mother added pictures of the ceremony to the walls of our sleeping chamber, they showed Heidl too.

Adding pictures of my ceremony will be more difficult, because of course it will take place in the spirit chamber, the first marriage ever celebrated there. Olaf and I would prefer to be married in darkness, to the sound of the stream, but Aunt Inge says the ceremony is for everyone. She wants a ring of torches around the entire group, with a single torch where we will stand, in our private place.

I have known since I was small that the spirit was strong there, but what was to occur at our wedding lies beyond any knowing.

AT MIDWINTER there are no flowers, but Folke and Mother and Aunt Inge cut evergreen boughs and weave them into wreaths—crowns for me and Olaf, and a large one surrounding us on the rock where we will stand. Folke shyly offers me a beautiful carved wooden bracelet she has worn most of her life; it was her mother's, and since Olaf was born she has intended it for his bride.

When I enter the spirit chamber with Mother and Father, the beauty of what I see astonishes me. The outer ring of torches lights every face, and dozens of sparkling pillars reflect flickering torches everywhere, receding into the far depths of the chamber. I have seen the spirit chamber every day since I was tiny, but never as it is today.

The children sit in a ring around the central torch, where Aunt Inge and Olaf wait. Angela sobs on Geyr's shoulder. Uncle Sigurd sits with his children, Fedr with his. Mother and Father lead me to Olaf and then sit with my brothers.

Aunt Inge begins by singing, as she did for Angela and Geyr. I don't know the language. Her voice is beautiful, and I am sure she is singing an ancient ceremonial song of her people. The song mingles with the sound of the stream, and as I stand facing Olaf I feel the connection that brought us here so strongly that when Aunt Inge finishes her song and begins speaking to us, I hardly hear what she says. When it is our turn to speak I am overwhelmed, tears filling my eyes as we say the ancient promises. Olaf takes my hands between his. Aunt Inge clasps our joined hands, and we stand in silence. The moment is frozen in my memory.

It is when the light begins.

At first I think I am imagining it, but no, the room is dimly lit now. A glow rises out of the stream and illuminates us all. A moment ago the torches were brilliant points of light in the dark; now they are all but eclipsed by the streamlight, as a rising dawn dims the stars.

Nobody moves or makes a sound, even the children. We are all transfixed. The light dims and brightens with the sound of the stream, and I realize I have seen it all along in some part of my mind. It is the light I have always used to find my way in the dark, now visible to all.

A miracle of the spirit.

Aunt Inge finds her voice first, long after the light finally dies away. "You are truly wedded in this holy place and by it. May you and your children and their children never forget this wonder." She turns to the group—our family—and proclaims us husband and wife. Still, no one moves for some time.

A few people eventually stir, but Aunt Inge holds up her hand. I have been so involved with Olaf and our wedding that I completely forgot that this midwinter also marks my coming of age—a milestone I've awaited for years.

Olaf moves aside to sit with Father, and Mother stands with Aunt Inge and me. They each pray for my health, happiness, and fertility. Mother speaks first, traditional words she heard many times as a child, perhaps so often that she didn't always reflect on their meaning, which strikes me with the force of a thunderstorm. I am a child no more, but an adult. I can expect sorrows and troubles as well as joys. I have an adult's responsibility to do my share and be kind and fair to others. I am a woman, with the duty and gift of bearing children and teaching them to be good adults in their own right. She said the same words when Angela came of age, but at eight I must have been too young to understand their meaning.

Aunt Inge tells me that my toughness, strength, and hunting ability make me my mother's equal, that she could offer no higher praise. She invites me to draw my own part of our story on the cave walls. She says she stood with my mother and grandmother in battle, that I am a worthy daughter and granddaughter to these heroic women and must always remember how much I have to live up to.

The praise embarrasses me, and I am relieved when she finally offers a criticism, with guidance: "You are too impulsive, Ana. You wanted to stay in Northpoint five years ago. Look what you would have missed. When you must make an important decision, think years ahead." She looks deeply at me and then goes on in a lower voice. "Most of all, Ana, you know the spirit of this chamber better than any of us. The light from the stream shows that. When you are older you will be our spiritual leader."

Grandmother sewed me a pouch of my own, to wear for the rest of my life; she gave it to Mother when I was eight, and Mother has kept it hidden from me for all that time. Inside are tiny figures. Father, remembering my fear of bears, carved a wooden bear to help protect me. Mother made a clay figure of a woman with a nursing infant. Aunt Inge carved a woman hunter with bow and arrow, and Uncle Sigurd a wolf.

Finally they hand me a figure carved from wood with a curly grain. I know the instant I see it that Olaf made it. With exquisite detail, it shows a man and woman, seated facing each other, knees and foreheads touching, arms wrapped around each other—actually through each other, the two figures becoming one.

The torches are burning low as we return to the sleeping chamber. Olaf and I put on boots and hooded capes and walk through ankle-deep snow to the cliff edge, with its moonlit view of hills descending to the distant seashore, and as we stand there it seems to me that we are looking along our own life path.

6

THE DREAMS BEGIN soon after the midwinter celebrations.

> *I am in Mother's village with Olaf. Mother and Father are with the village elders. People are saying Father and Uncle Sigurd stole Folke and I put a spell on Olaf to keep him with me. I explain that these are poisonous lies spread by Olaf's father, but no one hears, and I am in despair. Now I am separated from Olaf as well. Olaf's father approaches me with a knife, hatred on his face.*

I wake in terror in the dark of the spirit chamber and quickly light a torch. Nearby, Olaf writhes in his sleep. When I rouse him, he shakes, speechless with rage and fear. He too saw his father threaten me. We are so agitated that our efforts to calm ourselves are futile at first, and it is some time before the sound of the stream relaxes us.

The spirit chamber never feels dangerous, even now when it gives us dreams of wickedness. Better that we know. But am I strong enough to withstand such hatred? I shrink in fear when I remember the dream.

We find Aunt Inge near the cave entrance, playing with Kyle, her four-year-old son. She smiles as we approach and then looks at us, startled. She leaves her children and leads us back to the spirit chamber.

"Tell me the dream." She wants every detail. Who was it that ignored my explanations? Where did Olaf's father approach me? On the waterfront? Who else from the Benchland was in the village? What was the time of year? Could I see the moon? What was the weather?

"I must think about this," she finally says, "and I will come here alone for guidance. Ana, we will tell your parents and Sigurd, but not yet. It won't affect what we do; we can't travel in winter. Olaf, your mother need not know of dreams like this one, at least not yet. Think how they would upset her."

We sit quietly, and the sound of the stream soothes me. Aunt Inge is taking on some of my burden. Once again I wish I might someday have her strength and wisdom.

"Ana—both of you—you must not give in to fear." She hesitates and then adds, "Sometimes the most useful visions are those that do not happen. We must be sure what you dreamed doesn't occur. Treat the dream as a warning and heed it. And give me time to think, please."

AUNT INGE APPROACHES US the next afternoon. "If you're thinking of not going to the spirit chamber for your daily nap," she says, understanding everything as usual, "go anyway. Your dreams are our only warning, and the next dream won't upset you so badly, because you will be ready for it."

> We are in Grandmother Amena's house so I can present Olaf to her. We see her sitting, weeping. "Grandmother," I say, "it's Ana, come to bring you my husband, Olaf."

> She looks at me. "They say Sigurd and Zoan stole his mother and that you bewitched him. None of that is true, is it?"

> "No, Grandmother, it's a lie, told by Olaf's father. Olaf and his family stayed overnight with us. Olaf and I discovered that we share the same spirit being. Olaf asked to stay longer so he and I could get to know each other. His father attacked him and struck his mother down. He would have done worse if Uncle Sigurd hadn't prevented it. Olaf's father tried to attack Uncle Sigurd with a knife and went away threatening revenge. Olaf and his mother remained with us. Olaf and I were married at the midwinter full moon. I came of age

then too," I added. "I am wearing the pouch you made for me."

"I didn't think it was true." She looks less despairing. "But many have heard these lies, and some believe them."

As I glance out the window, I see smoke at the waterfront. I know that Olaf's father has burned our new boat.

By the time Aunt Inge hears this dream she has decided to tell Sigurd and my parents everything, in the spirit chamber this evening. She asks us to spend the evening with Fedr and Folke.

Adult responsibilities come in many forms, I see. Much depends on Olaf and me. Mother said it clearly: I can expect sorrows and troubles as well as joys. Even so, I am startled by how fast my life has changed. A few months ago, I was still a child.

THE DREAMS CONTINUE, but we find them less and less frightening, and we are happy to be side by side in this fight.

We are in the new boat, Father, Olaf, and I, fishing for the day. I love being on the ocean. Another boat approaches us. We see Olaf's uncle, waving. He is agitated as he comes alongside. He says Olaf's father is dangerous and we must be careful. He is ashamed of his brother's behavior, and the two of them no longer speak.

After he leaves, we talk about what he said. The wind drops, and Father tries to raise our second sail, but it has been cut to pieces in its bag.

Father and Uncle Sigurd are unsurprised by what the dreams have taught us. Uncle Sigurd says, "He revealed his meanness when he turned on you, Ana. I should have put an arrow through him then, as I wanted to. It would have saved us a great deal of effort."

"We have known since he left that we would have to confront him," Father says. "The dreams are invaluable. Without them we wouldn't know about the boat or about the lies he is telling in Northpoint."

THE WINTER IS A TIME OF WORK, for by spring we must have goods to trade for the new boat. Father and Uncle Sigurd lead the younger men. They put Olaf and Fedr to work chipping glarestone, while Geyr and Druian work with them at the small oven baking molds for redmetal—arrowheads, spear points, rings like Mother's, and copies of Heidl's engraved bracelets. Mother makes all the molds, and we need many; each is used only once. She soon exhausts her store of clay, and Geyr and Druian dig more from the spring, a hard job made harder by cold weather.

Once the molds are ready, Father and Uncle Sigurd spend days at the oven with Geyr and Druian, casting redmetal and then finishing the objects with hammers and smoothing tools.

This work requires large quantities of green gravel and firerock. Geyr and Druian take advantage of sunny days to haul both up to the bench from below. Olaf helps when they need it but spends most of his time working glarestone.

All the men are busy every day at this winter work, except when they are hunting.

For Angela, this time is a trial. She depends on Geyr's help with the six small children—Fedr's three, my little brother Aramel, and Eydis and Kyle, Aunt Inge's little ones. Now Geyr spends his days working, and we all suffer from Angela's unhappiness. At night I hear her argue with Geyr, her tone between an accusation and a whine. Aunt Inge and I help her by turns when we can, but we are often too busy. Aunt Inge's daughter Ragna is almost my age and has more time, but when she tries to help, Angela's crossness toward her quickly brings Druian into the fray—he adores Ragna and protects her fiercely. Ragna was my best friend until Olaf arrived, and I too chafe at Angela's harshness.

Angela resents my time in the spirit chamber. When Aunt Inge explains why it's necessary, Angela rolls her eyes, although never so Aunt Inge can see. When I was small, Angela always shifted her work to me if she could and was snappish and resentful when she felt her load was too high. Now she is constantly busy caring for small children and uncomfortable from pregnancy as well. Her impatience with the little ones even causes friction between her and Aunt Inge.

The wintertime work also brings out Druian's resentment of Olaf, perhaps for the time he spends with Father, but I recall that when Druian was learning glarestone work, he was bored. Olaf and Druian work together without conflict, but I know Druian well and can feel his rancor.

Druian's real interests are in hunting and Ragna. We all see that in time they will marry—neither would seek a mate outside the group. Druian is a strong and opinionated man, and I hope Ragna is not too meek to stand up to him. In any event, that marriage will be welcomed as part of the natural order of things, enabling our community to thrive.

Angela's ill temper is particularly hard on three-year-old Svala, Fedr's youngest, born of Heidl on the terrible night of her death. Svala's difficult birth resulted in a deformed foot, and she walks with a limp. Mother and Aunt Inge fear she might never succeed on her own. She does her best to run and play with the other children, but she is often left behind. She soothes herself by clinging to the nearest adult, normally Angela. Svala is desperate for love and comfort, but Angela frequently has harsh words for her, which drives Svala into inconsolable crying. That's when Aunt Inge steps in and tempers flare. Mother wisely refuses to take sides. She says Angela needs to see how her behavior affects others. I doubt Angela cares. I'm quite sure she won't change.

DESPITE ANGELA'S RESENTMENT, Olaf and I continue to nap in the spirit chamber in the late afternoon, after our work is done.

> *In Mother and Father's village, we head for the waterfront to check on our boat. A crowd surrounds us in the village square. I have never seen so many people in one place. An angry dispute erupts, with pushing and shoving and a feeling of threat and danger. Olaf and I are in the center of the fighting. I turn to Olaf, but he and the crowd are gone, and I am alone with his father, who advances toward me with a knife. I calmly prepare to fight. I feel no fear but know that even though I am younger and faster, I could die.*

When I was in the village five years ago, I loved the waterfront and went there almost every day to enjoy the ocean and watch the fishing boats come and go. The dreams all occur there or in the village square. Dreams like this one, shared with Olaf, come throughout the winter, thirty or forty within three months, all with similar messages. By the time we sail south, Olaf and I have encountered his father many times and have seen many pillars of smoke.

Spirit Chamber

Aunt Inge wants to hear the details of every dream. She and Mother are anxious for my safety, but Mother has always told me I would not be able to escape my fate. It was in the spirit chamber that I found my connection with Olaf, and I believe our dreams there are visions of truth. I find it curious that I don't usually fear Olaf's father in the dreams. Perhaps I am worthy of my hero mother, as Aunt Inge said when I came of age, or perhaps I'm merely a foolish young woman. But the man is a villain, a real one, violent and cruel, as in the old tales, and since the morning he aimed his hatred squarely at me, part of me has known it is my fate to face him.

7

FATHER AND UNCLE SIGURD spend many evenings discussing who should travel with us, but in truth there is little to discuss. Father and Mother will go so they can see their aged mothers, perhaps for the last time. Uncle Sigurd's reasons are like mine: he has felt since the morning Olaf's father threatened him with a knife that they would meet again. Aunt Inge will go because Uncle Sigurd is going. Olaf would go to be with me even if his father weren't a threat. Angela and Geyr will stay here because Angela is pregnant, Fedr and Folke because the children need care. My brothers present the only questions. Druian is sixteen, tall and strong, much like Father, and as good-natured. He would be a big help at home and in any case does not want to be separated from Ragna, which I understand. She has a loving heart and a fine sense of humor, and if I were Druian I wouldn't want to leave either. Aramel is four, and he is not going because Mother says not. So our traveling group will be six—Olaf and I plus the four elders. I feel quite grown up, a wedded adult woman, traveling with five people who are heroes to me.

Spring has come early, for once. The bench is nearly clear of snow, and the days are warm. We will leave in the morning. We hope the boat is ready as Karl promised. I am excited and nervous.

Olaf and I share one final dream, a little different from the many that came before.

> *A crowd has gathered around us. People point at me, crying, "Witch!" Smoke rises from the waterfront area, and I fear our boat is burning. Olaf's father walks out of the smoke toward me, a look of triumph on his face. "Burn her!" he screams. "She trapped him with magic! Burn her!"*

Somehow this awful dream doesn't bother me. If it had been the first, perhaps I would simply have given up, but after an entire winter of dreams I have resigned myself to my fate, and still I am confident I will live to bear Olaf's children. The dream horrifies the others, though, particularly Mother, and throughout the trip the elders quietly discuss it among themselves.

OUR DEPARTURE IS NOT PEACEFUL. Star barks and howls as the six of us descend to the village, and the children cry, except Eydis, who nestles happily next to Angela. "Listen to that dog," Aunt Inge says. "It was Lyna who howled when we first made this journey. Angela was a baby then," she adds, looking at me. "I was about your age. I feared what was to come and wasn't sure I would return. This departure is difficult too, because I am leaving my children behind."

We all have heavy packs. Father, Uncle Sigurd, and Olaf also carry spears with redmetal points. Bears are dangerous at this time of year, but if I am strong enough and emotionally tough enough to face Olaf's father, I need not fear bears. I know I will return home safely.

"Yes," Aunt Inge says. We are walking together behind the others. "The spirit makes you strong. Your shared dreams of prophecy have no hint of death. Only conflict." The instant she says it, I know she's right.

"I'm sorry I didn't grow up in the spirit chamber," she adds. "I would have gone there every day too. Even so, I could never have achieved what you have."

"Aunt Inge, how do you always know what I am thinking?"

She smiles. "We are so much alike."

Am I like Aunt Inge? That's what I've always hoped, but is it so? She knows so much and has such good judgment. If I live long enough to achieve her wisdom, I will use it to teach.

THE LAND CHANGES as we go, but everywhere the spring scenery is beautiful. The river roars with snowmelt from the mountains to the north. Near the bench, the land is beginning to show green shoots, and the trees have a few buds. Lower down, closer to Rivermouth, early flowers line the riverbank and the trees are already out in leaf. To Olaf, who has lived his life farther north, this scene is luxurious and verdant, like springtime in an old tale. I'm sorry he won't see spring on the Benchland this year, but we will have many years there to enjoy the season together.

We do see one bear, who simply looks at us from the other side of a raging torrent and goes his way. Otherwise the walk is uneventful. After the shock of my dream wears off, Mother relaxes and tells stories of the first trip, when Angela was a baby. To me, taking a baby on such a long trip sounds terrible, having to care for her and amuse her, but the four of them laugh about that long-ago time. Mother and Aunt Inge were terribly seasick on that boat trip and are anxious about the one ahead of us, even though we have an herb remedy from Aunt Inge's grandmother and another from Folke.

It is raining lightly when we arrive in Rivermouth, and we are relieved to see the boat in the water and tied to the walkway. The village is exactly as I saw it in my dreams, except that the burned hulk of the old boat is gone.

One of Karl's sons greets us. He and his brothers have worked on the boat all winter. They put it into the water six days ago. Father and Uncle Sigurd have no business to discuss; they made their bargain with Karl last fall. His son shows us the boat, which has four sails—one extra for each mast. Wooden storage shelves in the covered cabin hold spare rope and hides for repairs.

Karl's son opens our packet of trade goods and inspects our glarestone points and bracelets of redmetal. He shakes his head in wonder at the workmanship. The package seems small compared to the boat, but each represents a full winter's work for two men.

We meet Karl, an old man now, confined to a chair. He is a widower and looks used up, but what a talker! "Do you know?" he asks me and Olaf—"Do you know what they did? They saved us all! Without them we would all be dead! Of course you know the story?" I've known it all my life, and Olaf has known it for half a year, but we smile and let him tell it. "They came here just as you have and sailed south for a month in one of my boats. They arrived in Northpoint before the raiders and gathered an army of farmers and fishermen. They all hid in a forest as four hundred raiders charged up a hill to be slain on the hilltop or pushed off into the sea. Otherwise the raiders would have massacred everybody in sight."

"Not even two hundred," Uncle Sigurd growls.

"These two,"—Karl points to Mother and Aunt Inge—"planted crossed redmetal spears on the hilltop and terrified the raiders. They were afraid of women not much older than you are! I remember them very well."

He looks at Mother and then back to me. "You've got to be her daughter. Am I right?"

He looks at Olaf. "He's your father, the man who burned the boat? Ingvar told me last fall that you stayed behind. You two are married now? Long life and many children!" Later, Aunt Inge tells me that on the first trip Karl never said a word except for business dealings, but his wife talked nonstop.

We spend the night in one of Karl's rooms. Outside, the waves boom on shore, and water laps at Karl's walkway and our new boat.

MOTHER WARNED ME that on a long sailing trip a time comes when everyone is ready for the voyage to end. For us that happens about seven days into a twenty-three-day trip. The boat is comfortable enough, and we have clear weather and good winds, with fresh fish to eat and no seasickness—but the days are long, starting before dawn and ending only at dark. Father and Uncle Sigurd would sail on into the night if they could do it safely, and I am always relieved when they finally draw the boat onto the beach and tie it to a tree to keep it from sailing off by itself.

The first two days are exciting, sailing south with the narrowing sea east of us and then crossing to the mainland. After that we sail endlessly southward with open ocean west of us—all day, every day. We do take one day off, while Father and Uncle Sigurd repair the boat's steering hinge. Olaf and I spend that day hunting and return with two rabbits, which taste wonderful compared to either dried venison or fish.

I love the ocean, but next time, not so much all at once.

As we travel south, Olaf and I enjoy the changing scenery and warming weather, but as the trip nears its end I think more often of what awaits us when we arrive. We draw nearer to Olaf's father daily. We don't talk about the unpleasantness we expect, but both of us feel it.

Before Northpoint, we will go to Westharbor, a village farther south on the coast. Father has friends there, and from them we can learn the seriousness of the talk of kidnapping and witchcraft. If many people believe those lies, we will leave the boat in Westharbor and walk to Northpoint. Otherwise we will sail there, but we will have to guard the boat, in shifts; one couple will stay on the boat every night.

We spend our last night on the shore of a bay not far from Northpoint—the same place the raiders camped a few days before the battle, eighteen years ago. Across the bay, we can see the cliffs where the fighting occurred. In the morning, as we sail across the mouth of the bay and below the cliffs, I cannot escape the grim picture of men falling to their deaths. We pass by Northpoint, which looks just as it did when I was eight. In the early afternoon we arrive at Westharbor, which is much smaller, without a proper waterfront. We draw the boat onto the beach. While we secure it and set up camp, Father trots toward the village to find his friends. The rest of us rejoice that our long journey is behind us.

FATHER RETURNS WITH TWO MEN he knew as boys. He taught them to climb. In the battle against the raiders, both fought beside him. They treat our elders as heroes of legend and are jovial and kind toward Olaf and me. They bring goat meat and a sweet pudding, with ale to drink. The five men build a fine fire on the beach, and we drink tea and ale while the meat roasts. Sunset over the ocean is beautiful. After twenty-three days of traveling, it comforts me to sit around the warm fire with Father's old friends. I will never forget the food— goat meat and creamy pudding made from goat's milk and honey, exotic and rich compared to our diet on the bench.

Father's friends know Northpoint well and have heard what Olaf's father says. The lies outrage them, but apparently not many people believe.

Later in the warm evening, as the four older men talk, Mother and Aunt Inge lie on the soft sand with Olaf and me, watching the moon and stars. We talk about goats. Why don't we have them on the bench? We could start with kids, hoisting them in deerhides. We saw herds of goats near Rivermouth. Olaf's father and mother raised goats, and Olaf tended them. I think we will start raising goats when we return. Star, who herds everything that moves, will defend them and keep them from straying. We can have milk, cheese, meat, and maybe yarn. Olaf watched the entire process of making yarn, and thinks he can do it. We could weave cloth!

WE SLEEP UNTIL ABOUT MIDNIGHT and then sail north by moonlight, arriving in Northpoint before moonset, still well before dawn. We sleep again until first light. Then my parents and Olaf and I head for Grandmother's, finding the village square deserted. Uncle Sigurd and Aunt Inge stay to guard the boat.

I feel a flush of joy as I hug Grandmother. She looks exactly as I remember her, but she puts her hands on my shoulders, saying, "Oh! You are so changed." She smiles through tears. "I hardly know you, Ana. When you left I was afraid I wouldn't see you again."

I present Olaf, and we tell her his story. "I knew Andor was lying," she says, hugging me again, "but some believe him."

Grandmother says Father's mother is healthy but frail. Father and Mother leave to visit her. Afterward they will speak to the elders. Olaf and I cook a meal while Grandmother tells us of Olaf's father.

MOTHER AND FATHER RETURN in the afternoon, and we start for the waterfront as a group. In the village square many people recognize our elders, but the greetings are reserved compared to five years ago. Near the waterfront, a young man stops, looks at Father, and asks accusingly, "Did you steal Andor's wife? Is this his son?"

Father looks calmly at him. "You're too young to understand. Ask your parents what they think."

At the boat, Aunt Inge says, "We saw Olaf's father. He didn't come near us, but he watched from a distance."

"Zoan?" The voice comes out of the gathering dark.

Father peers through the gloom, and his face breaks into a smile. "Aodan! I feared I might not see you! Welcome!" Father leaps from the boat onto the walkway, clasps the arms of yet another old friend, and turns to the rest of us. "Aodan and I hunted together as boys, but we haven't seen each other for years. He was far away in the south at the time of our battle."

Aodan has little time for introductions. "I must speak quickly and leave. Andor is planning to confront you tomorrow morning in the square, with a group of his followers. Beware." He nods to us all and disappears into the evening.

Uncle Sigurd paces restlessly, as he does when he is thinking. He does not speak for some time. "His target is Ana," he says at last, "although he hates me too. If he will be in the square early with many friends, I don't want Ana in the village. She and Olaf can stay with the boat. The four of us will sleep in Amena's house and come to the square at first light."

Mother looks pained. "You would leave them to face Olaf's father by themselves?"

"If he comes, he would be alone. The walkway is too narrow for his friends. Ana and Olaf would have the advantage of darkness and would be expecting him. He wouldn't know what lay in wait for him."

Mother is silent, but I can see she is still not happy about the arrangements.

EIGHT MONTHS HAVE PASSED since Olaf and his family came to the Benchland. His father stayed less than a day but left a deep mark on my spirit. For those eight months he has darkened my dreams and given a face to my fears.

Uncle Sigurd's conviction that we must confront Olaf's father led us to spend a month at sea, but my own understanding comes from the spirit. It is I who will meet him.

Now that fated encounter is upon me. I am not afraid, although my heart tells me to be prepared for the worst. I would be foolish not to. He threatened to kill me in real life, and has attacked me repeatedly in dreams.

We have brought food from Grandmother's house, and the six of us eat as we plan what we must do. There is no further sign of Olaf's father.

8

OLAF AND I ARE SILENT and watchful after the elders leave the boat for Grandmother's house. Sleep is out of the question. The moon sets long before dawn, but the numberless stars provide better light than the spirit chamber ever sees. This scene is familiar from our dreams.

Our task is to watch the walkway from hiding as dawn breaks, in case Olaf's father comes here before we meet him in the square.

The waterfront's walkway—a narrow, floating structure that tilts underfoot—begins near the village square and runs south, slightly off the rocky shore. Almost three dozen boats are tied lengthwise along the seaward side—working fishing boats, all deserted. Our boat is tied near the far end. We leave the boat and walk to the village end of the walkway. We don't need a torch; our eyes have adjusted fully. We have our bows and arrows and our daggers as well, Olaf's with his own glarestone blade.

Talking in whispers, we lurk in the shadows of a storage shack. The long wait gives me time to think about how fast I have had to grow up. I was a child until Olaf and I discovered each other in the spirit chamber. Others have been forced abruptly into adulthood— Aunt Inge and Uncle Sigurd were both children when they lost their families to raiders, and Heidl was my age when she lost her brothers and her first husband, Geyr's father. Still, I am astonished. A year ago I could not have imagined myself unafraid and ready to face a madman who wants to kill me because he thinks I witched his son.

AT LONG LAST Olaf touches my arm and nods toward the village square. Someone carrying a torch comes toward us, passes our hiding place, and moves cautiously onto the walkway, heading in the direction of our boat—a man. Is he Olaf's father? In the dark, we can't tell. Olaf silently follows. I wait, as we agreed, in case more people appear.

Waiting alone, I grow anxious, and my heart pounds as the torch recedes down the walkway. I lose sight of Olaf. Behind the village, I see the first light of dawn over the hills to the east.

I also see that I am no longer alone.

A second man emerges from the village onto the walkway. He has no torch but feels his way carefully through the darkness. After he passes, I follow as quietly as I can. I feel sick; Olaf is trapped between the two men.

The torch is well down the walkway, near our boat, when the silence is broken by a shout and a scuffle from that direction, followed by a splash. The torch disappears. The figure in front of me sprints down the walkway. I run after him. The light is growing, but it is still too dark to tell what happened near the boat.

I STUMBLE IN THE DARKNESS, and the man I'm following stops and turns back toward me.

Olaf's father.

The face of my nightmares is twisted with hatred. "You!" he hisses.

He advances, knife in hand. I can't possibly fight him up close; he is too big and too heavy. On the other hand, I am faster on my feet and more nimble on the insecure walkway. We are still fifteen paces apart. I can escape by running, anytime up to the last instant.

I notch an arrow and draw my bow.

He stops, glaring at me. Does Olaf know yet that the man with the torch was not his father?

A blow from behind knocks me to my knees. My left arm is seized and wrenched, and I lose bow and arrow. I should have realized that Olaf's father might have another accomplice.

I snatch my dagger from my belt and strike blindly upward behind me. To my astonishment, I hear a gasp of pain, and I am free. I jump to my feet, but Olaf's father is upon me. He sweeps his knife horizontally, and blood spurts from my left arm. He lowers his shoulder and charges into me. I go down onto my back, dropping my dagger. He pins me down with his left arm while with his right he raises his knife.

I must fight back or die. I kick upward into his midsection and twist away with all my strength. His downward stroke buries the knife in the wood of the walkway.

He yanks the knife back and raises it again, but Olaf appears out of the darkness and grabs the upraised right arm from behind. The knife falls away into the water. His father turns and strikes at him left-handed, but Olaf seizes that arm and twists it viciously. I hear the arm snap.

Olaf lifts his father, throws him face down onto the walkway, leaps bodily upon him, and pulls his head back by the hair. I have seen Olaf kill deer, and I realize with horror that he is about to cut his father's throat.

"Olaf, NO!" My scream sounds out of control, but Olaf hears and hesitates.

I catch my breath. "He's not worth the pain it would cause you. I'm not badly hurt."

Olaf's father is reduced to a pathetic figure, his face bleeding, his arm broken, his anger and defiance gone. "Please," he says. "Please."

"I will kill you," Olaf says, "if you touch her again, or come near any of us."

"Please." Olaf's father begs for his life. "I'll leave. You'll see me no more."

Olaf stands, and his father staggers to his feet and walks brokenly toward the village. Olaf helps me up.

The man behind me lies motionless in a pool of his own blood, which has saturated his leggings. We kneel beside him. He is barely conscious and still losing blood fast. He draws a last gasping breath and is gone.

How do I feel about having killed a man? No guilt, no reaction of horror. I do not even feel regret; I was fighting for my life. I pick up my dagger and bow, but the arrow and Olaf's glarestone point are lost.

My arm wound is bleeding profusely but not gushing like the leg wound that killed my attacker. A wave of faintness sweeps over me, and Olaf half-carries me to the boat, where he washes and binds my cut— intensely painful in saltwater, our only choice. I feel stronger after I rest briefly.

The sun rises over the eastern hills as we leave the boat and head toward Grandmother's house.

AS WE TURN THE CORNER toward the center of the village, we see a crowd of young men milling around the square. They must have been here for some time; they cannot have assembled just since the attack on the walkway. Aodan warned us of this group. Has Olaf's father not told them he no longer wants to fight?

As they surge toward us, I see Olaf's father among them and hear his hateful voice. "Burn the witch!"

Another dream scene has become real.

We cannot fight twenty men, and already their number grows, as more are drawn by the commotion. The crowd comes closer now, out of control. Again I hear the voice of Olaf's father, straight from my dreams: "Burn her!"

"Burn her! Burn the witch!" Many join now, in a nightmare chant. The closest faces are distorted in mindless hatred. The crazed crowd is far worse than any dream.

Glancing at Olaf as he fits an arrow to his bow, I see what kind of man he is. His face shows neither fear nor panic, but anger and determined readiness for battle. How could this man I so admire be the son of such a coward?

ABRUPTLY, the clamor dwindles to silence.

I see no reason, but one by one, men stop their chant and look to our right. The gathering house blocks our view, but it is impossible not to follow so many shocked gazes, and we too are looking toward the gathering house when out into the square come our five elders.

Grandmother is in the middle, aged but walking on her own. Father and Uncle Sigurd carry their bows, with arrows notched but pointed downward. The three women carry redmetal-tipped spears and have let down their hair.

They are recreating the scene of eighteen years ago, when the five of them saved this village!

The morning is sunny, without the thunder and rain of that long-ago day, but the five bring history to life in a way every man in the square understands—not only the older ones; even the youngest knows every detail. Karl the boatmaker knows the story, far north of here.

The crowd stands stunned. Not a man moves.

The silence holds as the five walk into the square. It holds as they approach Olaf and me. It holds as they stand before us and turn to face the crowd.

Then Grandmother steps forward to speak.

"Shame!" Her voice is clear. "Shame! You forget so soon! You dishonor our village by believing Andor, who speaks only lies!" Her strength and presence grow as she speaks, and I see that Mother's deadly anger is a legacy from Grandmother.

"Know that Andor hurt his wife and son for years, until they escaped him. Behind me stands Sigurd, who led you to victory. He did not retaliate when Andor threatened him with a knife, and Andor's gratitude was to accuse him of kidnapping."

Grandmother turns and draws Olaf and me forward. She turns back to the crowd and places one hand on each of us. Her head barely reaches Olaf's shoulder. She looks at the crowd a long moment before continuing.

"Standing before the heroes who saved us, I present Ana, my granddaughter, daughter of Zoan and Quitana, and Ana's husband Olaf, son of Andor. Ana is of my blood and yours. To burn her you must burn me first. You behave like barbarians! *Shame!*"

GRANDMOTHER'S VOICE echoes off the walls surrounding the square. For a respected elder to speak in such anger is an extreme rebuke, and the crowd stands as though turned to stone.

A scream from the corner of the square breaks the silence, and I glimpse something flashing toward us. Olaf gasps and falls. I look in horror—blood is everywhere, and he is on his side, clutching at his neck, at a knife.

Uncle Sigurd and Father whip around, bows drawn. They are too late to take revenge on Olaf's father, for he lies face down, an arrow protruding from his back. Behind him, Olaf's uncle lowers his bow. He has killed his own brother.

Aunt Inge and Grandmother join me as I kneel over Olaf. He is bleeding from a deep cut. He tries to sit, but Aunt Inge gently holds him down while she removes the knife.

"You're lucky, Olaf. You're not badly hurt. Hold your hand to the wound. We'll bind it as soon as we have water." Later she tells me that if the knife had been one thumb closer to his throat it would have killed him.

As I help Olaf sit up, his uncle comes to us. "I didn't have time to warn you; he was too quick. For eight months he has hated you and spoken of nothing else. Only a few believed him, but everyone has heard his ceaseless lies. Ana, I think he was throwing at you. I feared he would kill you. May his spirit forgive me." He turns and walks away, head down, bow still in hand.

Andor's throw was wild because the arrow struck him as the knife left his hand. Olaf and I owe our lives to Olaf's uncle.

A chill of horror comes over me. How naive I was! Facing Andor on the walkway, I believed I could escape him by running! I did not think of a thrown knife.

The righteous anger of the crowd had crumbled even before they saw their leader disgrace himself with the knife attack. Now nothing remains but a few shocked and humiliated people, their bravery gone as cold as a campfire in a rainstorm. They all wander away, leaving the seven of us alone in the square with the motionless body of Olaf's father.

9

WE LEAD OLAF to Grandmother's house, where we clean and bind his wound. With the excitement behind us, we are hungry and exhausted. We eat, but before we rest, we must speak to the elders and visit Father's mother.

We go to the gathering house as a group of six; Grandmother spends the morning napping. The elders are discussing the matter when we arrive. Two of them saw what happened in the square. A messenger has already left to summon Olaf's uncle.

Father relates the story from the beginning—the episode at the Benchland and the first accusation of witchcraft, the burning of the boat, our learning of the talk of kidnapping—everything leading up to this morning's killings. Olaf and I tell of the attack by Olaf's father and two other men on the walkway.

The elders confer quietly before they respond. "Zoan, we rejoice that you and your family are not badly hurt. We did not understand until this morning that so many believed Andor." The spokesman knew Mother and Father as children and remembers Uncle Sigurd and Aunt Inge.

Mother, Olaf, and I go with Father to visit his mother, my grandmother Meriel, who barely gets around her house now. She is alone when we arrive, but her daughter—Father's sister—comes daily to help her. Grandmother Meriel is happy to see me and meet Olaf. She wants no ugly details but is glad we are vindicated and wishes us happiness.

We walk through the village square once more as we return to Grandmother Amena's house. By now the entire village knows of Andor's treachery, and those who believed his lies are nowhere to be seen. Mother and Father's old friends stop to talk, and we learn that the elders spoke to Olaf's uncle and held him guiltless, but asked him to take Andor's body.

We still don't know the identity of the third man on the walkway—the one who carried the torch. After Olaf pushed him into the water, he must have crawled out over the rocks.

We are spent, all of us. We nap, eat, and talk with Grandmother. At dawn tomorrow, we will visit the battle memorial on the hilltop. I saw it six years ago with Mother and Father. This time all five elders will go, including Grandmother. She complains that the hilltop is higher every year, but it is sacred to her, and she will go there until the day she no longer can. All my life I've heard about them standing on the hilltop, surrounded by the bodies of raiders. Tomorrow they will stand there together again for the first time since the battle, and I will cherish the memory forever.

This morning, my eyes filled with tears as they came into the village square five abreast. Heroes, all of them.

OLAF AND I TELL GRANDMOTHER about our dreams and about the spirit chamber—how it brought us together, and how the stream lit the chamber when we married.

Grandmother looks sharply at us but remains silent for a time before she speaks. "The spirit marked your union by revealing itself to everyone," she says at last.

Aunt Inge says, "Quitana and I have felt for years that Ana will be our spiritual leader."

Grandmother looks at her and nods, and then holds both my hands. "The light from the stream shows that your marriage is important to your people. It means your children will follow you in the path of the spirit. I saw the spirit in you before, but you were so young! I could only hope you would grow as you have."

"She has gone to the spirit chamber almost every day of her life," Mother says.

Grandmother looks deep into me. "Ana, you're grown and wedded now and will soon have your own children. Even so, you must continue to visit that sacred place." She turns to Olaf and adds, "You must help her."

Grandmother is wise and wonderful, and I am saddened by knowing that this is undoubtedly my last visit with her.

"You must not be sad! We have no idea what to expect when our lives end." She understands what I am thinking as well as Aunt Inge does.

I am sad, though—sad that I will have only a little time with her before we return home. I think of her eighteen years ago, defying her husband to stand in battle beside Aunt Inge and my young mother. Aunt Inge was right. I have much to live up to.

In the late afternoon, Olaf's uncle comes to Grandmother's house. He greets the elders courteously and then turns to Olaf and me.

"I want you two to have Andor's boat."

Grandmother is listening. "They have no way to use a boat, Ingvar. They live far inland."

Could we use another boat to travel north by ourselves? How would Olaf feel about that? Unexpectedly, I break down, sobbing.

Mother comes to my rescue. "Ana, your tears say you would like to stay longer with your grandmother."

Olaf's uncle smiles. "They could use the boat to return later. When they arrive in Rivermouth, they could trade the boat to Karl. He will be happy to have it. I'll tell him about it—many boats sail north from here, and I'll send a message."

This is my last visit with Grandmother, my last chance to learn from her. Without reason, I feel overwhelmed and clutch Olaf for comfort and support. For months my life has been centered on the tension of our quest and our fight, and without it I feel rudderless. A longer visit is exactly what my heart wants.

How does Olaf feel? Could we be happy away from the spirit chamber for that long? We look at each other and walk outside. I don't even have time to voice my question. "We could sail in late summer, or even next year. The spirit chamber will be always be there. She will not. We should stay with her if she will have us. We can help her."

Aunt Inge joins us. "Ana, you should stay. She will teach you. And she needs you. She's too old to live alone. You could care for her."

GRANDMOTHER'S MIND works like mine. "I hoped you would stay. We can teach each other. I need to know more of the spirit chamber, and you will come to know the spirit of the hilltop we'll visit tomorrow."

Now it is Mother's turn to cry. I see her and Grandmother in a long silent embrace. When I approach her later to sympathize, she smiles. "Until you decided to stay, I couldn't cry. I was horror-struck by the thought of leaving Mother alone and never seeing her again. I asked your father if he thought I should stay. He said to stay if I needed to, but I can't. I have a four-year-old at home and a grandchild coming. I'll miss you, but my mind will be at peace."

The paintings on the walls here show Mother and her sisters as children. I know Mother better for seeing them. I will be richer for living in this house.

THE WALK TO THE HILLTOP is hard for Grandmother, but I can see the place nourishes her spirit. The five elders stand at the cliff edge looking west over the ocean, the picture I've wanted to see since I was small, although I know it already from the paintings on the cave wall. Mother has described the battle to me so clearly that I can almost remember being here myself. She is lost in her memories, standing arm in arm with Father. Aunt Inge and Grandmother show me the spring where they cared for the wounded men. At the cliff edge, Olaf stands with Uncle Sigurd, whose gestures show that he too is talking of that day.

The two crossed spears are now part of a memorial to the local fighters who died here. "My spear disappeared in the lightning bolt that turned the battle," Grandmother says. "I can feel three spears here still. These two will decay with time. Mine will be here forever."

Mother, Aunt Inge, and Grandmother start back down toward the village, but Olaf and I ask Uncle Sigurd and Father to show us the details of the battle—where Father's and Uncle Sigurd's men waited in the forest and where the man was struck by lightning as he held Grandmother's spear aloft in triumph. We stand where Mother and Aunt Inge and Grandmother stood as the raiders ran uphill toward them, warrior women whose bravery is my heritage.

Standing on the cliff edge before we return to the village, looking down on the waves crashing onto the rocks far below, I feel a chill of horror, feel the terror of the men who were pushed off the cliff to their deaths. This hilltop has power, as the spirit chamber does, but it is not a place of peace. Grandmother comes here whenever she's strong enough. She says it fills her with energy.

The hilltop also gives us a view of the rooftops of Northpoint, where as a child I wanted to live because I couldn't imagine how else I would meet a husband. Now I will live there to care for Grandmother and learn from her. Olaf and I will return to the Benchland and the spirit chamber soon enough, before we have children. Meanwhile we'll stay where my parents grew up and are heroes.

It must be part of my fate, this village where Olaf's father tried to kill me.

The boat trip north—almost two months alone with Olaf—was wonderful, but I'm glad to be through traveling. The boat is equipped for fishing, and we caught and ate fish throughout the trip. Olaf sailed with his uncle often during our year in Northpoint and became an accomplished fisherman.

We expect to walk to the Benchland by ourselves, but to our astonishment Uncle Sigurd and Aunt Inge are waiting for us at Rivermouth. "I have dreams of my own, you know," Aunt Inge says, after the happy embraces. "Your mother would have come with us, but she is tending Angela's son. I also bring Folke's love to both of you."

Karl's sons also greet us, and we learn that they have taken over the business. "Is this Ingvar's boat," one asks, "that you will leave with us? We would be happy to have it."

We trade regularly in Rivermouth, and when Father and Uncle Sigurd next come here, they will strike a bargain with Karl's sons. Perhaps the boat will bring us the bullock and cart Father has desired since I was a little girl.

While we unload the boat and prepare our packs for the walk home, Aunt Inge and I talk. "I dreamed of Amena's death," she says. "I remember her anger in the village square last year and her courage and strength on the hilltop twenty years ago. She will be part of me forever."

"She was happy to her last day. She gave me more in a year than I could ever have gained otherwise. She taught me to be an adult and to nurture my spirit self. She freed me and Olaf from his father's tragedy. We needed that, and she needed to teach it. We buried her at dawn on the hilltop, as she wanted."

I have trouble going on, as always when I think of that day, and I continue through tears. "Afterward we stood in the forest in the rain as lightning struck her grave."

Aunt Inge hugs me. Then she draws back to look at me and exclaims, "You're pregnant!" Olaf laughs, as he does every time he thinks of it.

"I'm due about midwinter. Grandmother gave me her pouch for our baby."

"We'll have two midwinter babies. Ragna also. I married her and Druian at midwinter, a year after you. We talked about you, and the light from the stream."

Aunt Inge looks at Olaf. "It was a double ceremony, with Fedr and Folke. Fedr saved her from terrible grief—she cried for a month after she heard how Andor died." Olaf is startled and then delighted. And we had worried that his mother would not recover emotionally!

THE WALK HOME from Rivermouth gives me five days to reflect on everything that has happened in the two years since Olaf arrived. Life on the bench didn't stop because we were gone, and soon all the children I grew up with will be adults too. I've thought often this year about adulthood, and about what Mother and Aunt Inge said when I came of age. I was one person before Olaf arrived, another after we found each other, and a third after the fight and the death of his father. Grandmother taught me that I am one person with all those as part of me. Now I will change again, with a baby. I must develop my spirit, love my husband and my elders, do my share, and prepare my children to do the same. For Olaf's father, life was never right. I'm glad he's gone, but I sympathize with his torment, so different from the richness of my life.

As I think of the day Olaf appeared in my life, a question forms in my mind, and a suspicion. I hurry forward to catch up to the group. Aunt Inge sees the puzzled look on my face and stops to talk. The men walk on ahead.

"Aunt Inge, when Olaf first arrived, why did Mother let me disappear into the cave for the afternoon with a boy she didn't know? I'm surprised she didn't interfere."

Aunt Inge says nothing at first. She points out a row of ducklings behind their mother, all sailing serenely downriver. I realize she is thinking about what to say, and my suspicion grows.

"She would have interfered," Aunt Inge says at last. "I told her you would be safe."

"You knew all along, didn't you? You saw Olaf and me as we are now! That's why you invited him to climb with you. It was *you* who brought us together."

Another pause. "Not I, but the spirit. Talking to Olaf and his family by the river that day, I felt that the spirit had brought him to you. When I saw the two of you together at the edge of the cliff, I knew."

AS THE BENCHLAND COMES INTO VIEW high above the river, Aunt Inge breaks into a trot and is first up the rope. In moments the clifftop is crowded. Olaf and I and Uncle Sigurd are still some distance behind. Star's barking turns to cries of delight when she recognizes me, and I am heartstruck by love for her, for my people, and for the place—Benchland, cave, spirit chamber, all of it. I am overwhelmed by my feeling of returning home.

PART TWO

INHERITANCE

I LOVE MY WORK, but this job has not gone well. Today was my sixth and last day photographing ice caves in Lava Beds National Monument for a documentary. Lava Beds is in high desert in the far northeastern corner of California. A lovely place for cavers, with miles of lava flows that include hundreds of lava tubes—but very cold in winter. Why would anyone arrange such a shoot in February, when it's even colder outside than in the ice caves?

I'm headed for the Klamath Falls airport after living for a week in a poorly-insulated trailer, where I worked on pictures nightly until midnight and then lay awake, listening to the howling wind outside. Today I worked in a cave until noon, changed into jeans, and stuffed my absurd collection of caving gear, cameras, tripods, computers, lights, and cables into my rental car. I will change planes in Portland and won't arrive in Baltimore until five in the morning.

The ice caves are beautiful, although threatened by warming weather, the subject of the documentary. The staff was great, from cavers to clerks. The problem is me. Two days into the job I had an upsetting dream of a cave that knew I was there. It had some power over me, and I was frightened. The dream still haunts me, and since that night nothing has been right. I've had the feeling that something is coming, or perhaps that I must do something. I've been distracted enough to make errors on routine photo setups.

Caves always affect me, and some disturb my dreams. A scary cave dream during a caving trip is not completely out of character.

Driving away from Lava Beds, I begin to feel more human, and by the time I reach Klamath Falls I'm hungry enough to stop for a sandwich. I skip the beer; I've learned not to start drinking when I'm unhappy. I arrive at the airport ahead of time, check my three large gear boxes, and buy a book for airplane reading. I never open it, because I sleep away most of the long flight from Portland to Baltimore, and although the sun is rising when I drive up to my condo, I feel completely myself for the first time in days. The nagging feeling of unfinished business has left me.

AFTER I SHOWER AND SLEEP a few hours, I begin working my way through a mountain of correspondence. I hear a voicemail from a lawyer in Stockholm, who asks me to call him collect. The business day has ended in Sweden, so I have all night to wonder what his call could be about. A lawyer? Sweden? I can't guess.

When I reach him, he tells me I have inherited some land from relatives I didn't know existed—a great-aunt and great-uncle. The property is a large landholding in Sweden that includes several square miles of mountainous terrain adjacent to a river. My benefactors intended to do something with the land, but gave up that idea late in their lives. The property has caves. They wanted it to go to a caver, and I guess I am the only one in the family. The lawyer says he knew them for years—wonderful people, extremely concerned about putting the property into good hands. He assures me the transaction will be straightforward. I can expect mail soon.

The package arrives a few days later. It contains the paperwork, a CD of maps and aerial photos, and a sealed letter from my benefactors.

To Mr. Jarrett Eriksson:

By the time you read this, you will have heard from our attorney and learned about the land we have bequeathed to you. This letter is to prepare you in advance for what you will find there.

The property was once part of a Swedish estate. It belonged first to the Crown and then to a succession of noble houses. We received it as a wedding gift in 1937. We explored it by car and on foot, and enjoyed its scenery and small caves.

The property includes a large shelf of inaccessible land, high on the west side of the river. In 1955 we hired a helicopter to take us there. The shelf is nearly five kilometers long, but quite narrow. It is a beautiful place, with an exceptional view, but its most important feature is a large cave, which is spectacular and unknown. We briefly entered the cave and were astonished to discover that it contains a profusion of artifacts of prehistoric people. We feared that if we made the cave public it would quickly be spoiled, and we have kept its existence secret.

We have read some of your writings on caves and caving, and we greatly admire your photography. Even before we confirmed that we are related to you, we believed you to be the right person to assume ownership. We are confident that you will recognize the cave's cultural value and treat it with respect.

A cautionary note: you may find visiting the cave a psychological burden. Fifty years have passed since our single visit, and for all that time, the cave has regularly and insistently appeared in our dreams. We are both scientists by profession.

I mention this so you will understand that we are objective thinkers and have not come lightly to our belief that the cave was in some way aware of our visit.

With highest regards,

Ingvar and Irma Eriksson

Right away I think of my own frightening dream experience with a cave that was—how did they put it?—aware of my visit. Out of curiosity, I replay the lawyer's original voicemail message.

The call came in on the first of March. The same night I had the dream.

NATURALLY, I want to visit the cave, and the sooner the better. I will take two caver friends, a married couple. She's a professor of anthropology who specializes in early human settlements. OMG, her email says, that's incredible, it might even have Paleolithic paintings. I am SO excited.

The arrangements take a full day and dozens of emails and phone calls. The longest trip we can all manage is one week in mid-April—two days flying, two days driving, three days underground. If the cave is as good as we hope, we'll arrange a longer expedition later.

I contact realtors to gather information. One of them knows the area well. "This place you describe—it is useless and inaccessible. Why are you interested?" I didn't actually care about his evaluation of the site; I simply wanted to know how to get there. The call is not useless, because he tells me about a quarry operation that owns the land between the river and the shelf—the only nearby land west of the river that does not belong to me. I thank him politely, and when the call ends each of us thinks the other is an idiot.

I have absolutely no clue about what lies ahead.

WE LUG ALL OUR STUFF to the airport and—much later— from the Stockholm airport into a rented SUV. The next morning, we drive far up the coast to the tiny town of Rivermouth. From there we turn upriver.

The canyon road is slow but beautiful, with spring flowers blooming beside the river. We drive almost three hours north and west. I recognize the place right away from the photos—a big broad shelf on the left side, hundreds of feet above the river. Flowers line a small waterfall that cascades from the shelf.

We stop to look, and I shoot pictures from the road. The top half of the climb looks vertical, but that's not a problem, because we won't be climbing it. When I contacted the quarry company last week they politely refused to allow us to reach the shelf through their property, saying that their operations make public use of the area unsafe. We will come down from above. That's easier in any case. Climbing big walls is not my thing.

The topo map shows a road farther upriver that ascends a tributary stream. We find it easily, about five miles north of the quarry, but 'road' is generous. 'Jeep track' comes to mind, but even that stretches the truth. It is extremely steep in places and deeply rutted. Our Subaru is barely tough enough. From the headwaters of the stream, we struggle up an impossibly steep slope to a ridge where we find patches of snow. This is the high point of the road; ahead of us, it descends to the southeast for miles. All on my property.

The GPS shows us only three miles west of the shelf, at about the same elevation, but on the opposite side of a north-south ridge that reaches high above us. We park the car and spend the afternoon carrying our stuff up the ridge to the mountaintop above the shelf— climbing rigs, ropes, caving suits, food, water, beer, first aid supplies, camera gear, and miscellaneous caving stuff. Two trips for each of us. We work hard until sunset. Perhaps the physical labor helps fight jet lag.

We pitch the tents at the mountaintop, with a view over the hills east of the river to the sea, forty miles as the crow flies; our driving route up the river was much longer. The entire shelf is laid out below us. It's bigger than I had expected, and heavily forested.

We cook steaks, and after dinner we drink beer and fantasize about what we will find tomorrow. The solstice is still two months away, but this far north the evenings are long even in April. When it finally gets dark, we can see the lights of several towns in the distance. Later a dazzling moon rises, and as I drift toward sleep I cannot believe this place belongs to me.

ROGER KRAMNICK AND I have been caving buddies since college, at Johns Hopkins. His wife Mira—Dr. Kramnick—is now an associate professor there. They're both small people with good caving builds. Roger is a softie, a warm and gentle man, but Mira is made of nails and fire. She's the real thing—the legendary tough Polish woman. She came to Baltimore straight from Krakow. She met Roger her first semester, and from then on our caving trips included her.

Roger is a geologist; he works for the federal government in Baltimore. I have a geology degree too, but I earn my living as a freelance caving journalist and photographer, my solution to the threat of growing up to do something other than caving. At first it was a thin existence, but after twenty years I have a full schedule of caving trips and can pick the ones I like best. To carve out this week I had to find someone else to cover an expedition to Hawaii to photograph lava tubes on the Big Island.

IN THE MORNING, we choose a tree above the midpoint of the shelf and rig the descent. From the topos I had estimated the drop to be 300 feet. It's actually more like 400, but we have plenty of rope. The rappel is easy. I'm down first; they lower the gear to me before descending. We are all on the shelf by ten.

The shelf is three miles long. The cave is probably at the base of the cliff, but might be concealed in the forest. We split into two search parties; Roger and Mira go south while I go north. We agree to return to the rappel rope and not enter the cave until we're all together.

The walk to the north end of the shelf and back takes more than an hour. The scenery and views are beautiful, and I shoot many pictures, but I find no cave. The rock wall drops from the mountaintop straight to the shelf all the way to the north end. Returning, I hug the edge of the cliff, a sheer drop to the river for its entire length.

I expect to hear that Roger and Mira found the cave, but they too have come up empty. They did find a big breakdown pile that could be hiding the cave entrance, at the base of the mountain wall near the south end of the shelf. We walk there to investigate. The breakdown looks forbidding. A stream flows out of it. Once there may have been a cave opening here, but all that remains is a giant pile of rock. Sharp edges suggest that the rockfall is recent, as it must be if my great-aunt and great-uncle found a cave entrance here in 1955.

We walk around the base of the breakdown. The stream emerges vigorously into a shallow canyon that deepens before it reaches the cliff edge, at the top of the waterfall we saw.

Finally, near the south end of the breakdown, I feel the airflow. If it blows, it goes. We've found the cave.

We clamber over the breakdown to find the source of the airflow and mark it. Then we return to the rappel rope for the gear. We bring the beer, but not the water; filtered stream water will be fine, and the stream will keep the beer cold too. It is two o'clock before we finish.

The day has already been long, and we're jet-lagged, but we are all eager to see the cave, so Roger and I set to work with our big pry bar. With an hour's work we move enough rock to reveal an open area behind the breakdown. A cool breeze blows from it. After another hour we have a hole big enough to crawl through.

This is the moment. We suit up and shoot pictures of ourselves in front of the cave entrance. Then we drop to our knees and crawl.

WE FIND OURSELVES in a tall room with no cave adornment, dimly lit by openings high in the breakdown. I see that this cavern was once open to the shelf, probably a nice place, a shady refuge in summer and dry in winter. Trees and shrubs grew here once, but they have withered and died in the half light.

The chamber ends a hundred feet back at a solid wall, with an obvious chest-high passage leading beyond. We walk toward it and are about to pass through when Mira stops and points. On one side of the chamber is a carefully-made rock structure the size of a washing machine, still mostly intact. An altar? We can't tell. I start toward it, but Mira shouts, "Jarrett, *stop!* Don't you dare touch it. Don't touch *anything!*" When she is excited her English becomes almost unintelligible.

Mira lays out a narrow red-tape pathway to the rock structure, to minimize the damage we do by walking. She examines the structure and points out fire scars. Then she puts on gloves and carefully pokes around in the charred dirt while I shoot pictures. She picks something up and brushes off a layer of dirt and ash, revealing a dark green chunk the size of a fingertip. Mira drops it into a sample bag, writes a label, records a note by speaking into her phone, and shows the bag to Roger and me.

"Look at that. Copper, I think. I can forget Paleolithic art. The people here were much more recent. This is a smelting oven."

Our caving trip is now an anthropological research project, with Mira in charge. She fishes in her pack and brings out gloves and plastic booties for all of us.

Before I duck through the entrance, I look back to shoot a picture of the ancient oven and the breakdown. People worked metal at that oven—people like us, but long ago. Who were they? When were they here?

12

WHEN I WAS SMALL, I loved to watch Mother paint the walls of the sleeping chamber. She worked slowly and carefully, using mostly red and black. Those are Grandmother's colors—Mother's mother, Grandmother Quitana. She and Aunt Inge covered one entire wall with their stories, and some of the back wall. Mother's paintings cover the rest of the back wall and part of the opposite wall. If Aunt Angela and Aunt Ragna paint even half as much as Mother and Grandmother and Aunt Inge, the sleeping chamber will be full, and there will be no place for my own story.

"Where will we paint when the walls are full?"

Mother answers with a twinkle in her eye. "We'll find someplace, Alys. I promise."

Mother says when she was small she worried about where she would ever find a husband. What I worry about is where I will paint my pictures. The pictures are important. Without them there will be no trace of us when we are gone.

"Grandmother, where will we paint pictures once the walls are full?" She bends to hug me and winces because her back hurts, but she doesn't stop smiling. "Not many eleven-year-olds think ahead like that." She looks seriously at me. "A girl smart enough to ask that is smart enough to figure out an answer."

When I ask Father, he laughs and lifts me high over his head, but Mother shouts at him. "*Olaf!* She's too big for that!" He smiles at her as he puts me down. "I don't know, Alys," he says. "I think you will learn the answer in the spirit chamber."

THREE OF US are about the same age. I turned eleven at midwinter. So did my cousin Astrid, Aunt Ragna's daughter, but I am one day older. My cousin Bjorn will be thirteen at midsummer, a month from now. We spend a lot of time together. I ask them about painting on the walls. Astrid asks her grandmother, Aunt Inge, who says, "I'll bet that question comes from Alys, doesn't it?" Then she winks at me. I love Aunt Inge.

I love all my family, but no one takes this question seriously but me. I know every one of Grandmother's paintings, and Aunt Inge's, and Mother's. I know the stories that go with them, but the pictures make them real for me.

I haven't even heard all the stories. Mother and Father don't talk about his father. When I ask, they say the story would scare me and can wait until I'm grown up. But it's right there in Mother's paintings. Does she think I can't see? She simply doesn't want to talk about what happened.

AT THE SPRING CELEBRATION in the spirit chamber, Mother sang a special prayer for our elders—Grandmother Quitana and Grandfather Zoan, Grandmother Folke and her husband Fedr, and Aunt Inge and Uncle Sigurd. Aunt Inge and Grandmother Quitana had taught Mother two different versions of the prayer, but she sang one of her own that she learned in the spirit chamber. The song was so beautiful it made me cry. I think everyone cried, and I could hear the spirit in the voice of the stream. When Mother sings, the spirit sings with her.

When I ask Grandmother Quitana whether she heard the spirit song, she smiles. "Not as well as you, Alys." Aunt Inge—Mother's teacher—says that until I was born Mother knew the spirit best, and now that's my job.

Today, as I sit in my place in the spirit chamber, I can tell I'm not alone. Listening to the stream, I understand that something unusual is about to happen. I don't know what or why.

I find Mother and Aunt Inge working in the garden. "I was alone in the spirit chamber and felt someone else there with me. What does that mean?"

"Alys, you will have to tell us what it means." Aunt Inge has picked some flowers, and leans over and puts two in my hair, above my ears.

Mother holds out her hand. "Let's go there together. Maybe I can feel it too."

So Mother and I are together in my spot in the spirit chamber. And I still feel someone else here.

WE FINALLY TURN ASIDE from the smelting oven and duck through the opening at the back of the entry chamber into almost-complete darkness. I turn on my helmet light and look around. The room is plain, like the entry chamber, but much bigger, perhaps 300 feet long by 200 wide.

People lived here. Many people; I see four substantial cooking hearths. Mira walks slowly toward the nearest hearth, laying down her red tape path as she goes. She is so busy making sure Roger and I don't touch anything that I see the paintings first.

Mira quickly follows my gaze to the walls. "Ohhhhh—my—God—"

We stand in shocked disbelief, turning slowly, using the LED mag lights to see around the chamber. Paintings cover all the walls, hundreds of feet of them. We spend the next hour touring the walls, Mira in the lead, laying red tape. She compares details to show us that the paintings are the work of several different artists. I have never seen her so excited.

"Look! This painter used blue, green, and yellow, and drew these soft lines and sexy curves. That one painted in red and black, and used strong strokes and big areas of color. They used each other's colors for accents. They had to be contemporaries. The back wall has more red and black paintings, but from another artist. These paintings span many years. The colors are from plant dyes. I can carbon date them."

She is beside herself. Years later she would tell me that seeing the paintings was the high point of her career.

I WILL NEED ALL DAY TOMORROW to photograph the paintings. For now I shoot video around the chamber, lit by Roger and Mira's mag lights. Mira finds more and more to say about the paintings. One shows the shelf outside, with a view of the sea, but with a substantial garden, including a plot of growing grain. Another shows a boy twisting plant fibers into thread, and one shows men pouring molten metal into a mold. "Copper Age," Mira says, "Late Neolithic. Five or six thousand years ago. I wonder—why were they in a cave? Many settlements from that period, not too far from here, were villages. You know, where people could live in real houses? Whatever. This is unprecedented. A scientific gold mine. It's so pure."

After I finish the video panorama and shoot pictures of the chamber overall and the four hearths, we pause to talk and take stock. In addition to the hearths, the chamber contains the remains of wooden objects, decayed almost to dust. We can't even tell what they might have been. We find a cracked obsidian spear point. People lived on both sides of the stream, which emerges from the west wall and runs roughly down the middle of the chamber, coursing from side to side. "They surely lived outside in summer," Mira says.

We all realize this cave is a Swedish national treasure that we have no right to keep to ourselves. But we don't have to reveal it right away. We aren't random members of the public. We're cavers and scientists, fully qualified to do the preliminary assessment of the cave. Of course if we're not careful, there will be hell to pay.

This chamber looks long untouched. I don't know how far my great-aunt and great-uncle came into the cave, but I see no trace of their visit. I suspect they were the first visitors for thousands of years.

Mira says she will need weeks to document this room alone. That can't happen on this trip, so we move on.

We walk to the back of the chamber, where an easy passage leads farther west. If we stop here, I could leave the cave without getting crazy. But I don't know that, so we press on.

WE FOLLOW MIRA as she crawls steeply upward. I hear her startled gasp before I can see anything but the rock of the tunnel-like passage. She stands and looks around. "Oh, God. Look at this."

Moments later the three of us stand at the top of a breakdown pile, overlooking a very different chamber, a dreamlike fantasy. The stream flows through this room too, winding between tall stalagmites, many of them full columns. A deep pool lies at the foot of our breakdown pile. The ceiling has stalactites and forests of soda straws. Every surface looks like gypsum, and everywhere I look, our helmet lights reflect back to me.

This chamber has a distinct presence. The three of us have felt something similar in the sacred cenotes in the Yucatan, near Tulum, the ruins of a Mayan temple, but there the feeling is oppressive, perhaps because those caves saw human sacrifice. This room feels benevolent. Protective.

It also feels occupied, as if someone else were here with us.

We clamber down to the pool, where a sturdy stone hearth squats at the foot of the breakdown. Mira examines it briefly. "Not for cooking. Only light and warmth. This room might have been a ceremonial chamber." Above the hearth, smoke has stained the ceiling. Otherwise the tenants left no marks here. They lived in the chamber with the four hearths. This was their temple.

We sit on a large flat rock beside the stream for an energy bar break and take in the stunning cave scenery as we talk about the best way to use our remaining two days. We are all exhausted. It is eight in the evening, time to exit the cave and set up camp. Tomorrow Roger will help Mira with a preliminary inventory of the living chamber while I photograph the paintings. We won't have time on this first trip to explore the rest of the cave.

Roger rises to leave.

"Wait," I say. "I'd like to kill the lights and stay a little longer. There's a feeling here, like in the cenotes."

Roger sits down without a word, and his is the last light to go off.

This is the moment of no return. In the dark, the stream seems louder—almost seductive—and I realize we are definitely not alone.

TIME PASSES, but I am too immersed in the experience to notice, and eventually it is ever-practical Roger who breaks the silence. "We could be here all night." He turns on his light and stands, and we leave the cave without a word, each of us lost in thought. We have work to do—unpack, make camp, fix dinner. Even as we eat, we talk only about other things—car needs gas, cold here at night. No one says a word about the ceremonial chamber.

Finally, I clean up the dishes and join Roger and Mira at the tents. They have a fire going.

"So." Mira sounds impatient. "What happened in there?" They have clearly been waiting for me before starting the discussion.

"We weren't alone." Roger is ever the dispassionate observer.

"One of the early people." Even the memory jolts me.

Mira looks sharply at me. "Man or woman?"

"Woman." Roger and I say it together.

Mira shrugs. "Me too."

What we have here is more than an inheritance, and more than an archaeological discovery, and more than a caving trip. We're in the midst of a real-life paranormal experience. Trained scientists, all of us.

WE DEVOTE OUR SECOND DAY to inventory and photography in the living chamber. I take more than a thousand pictures, and Mira collects many dozen samples. Like all cave tasks, the photography takes twice as long as I expect and is three times as tiring. At day's end we spend an hour at the west end of the living chamber, where I make minutely-detailed macro photos of the two nearby hearths as Mira and Roger methodically collect samples and make notes. Mira has one of my cameras and photographs every object in place before she moves it.

Tomorrow morning Mira will continue to work here while Roger and I begin a survey of the rooms we've seen. Then we'll run for home. Thinking that plan through, I realize we haven't left time for photos of the ceremonial chamber, the scenic climax of the cave. Without those shots the trip will be incomplete. The day has been long, but I'm not too tired to devote an hour to pictures of such a place.

I load camera, tripods, flash units, and an LED floodlight into my pack, tell Roger and Mira where I'm going, and start up the tunnel.

ONCE AGAIN, the inner chamber's sheer beauty brings me to a standstill. I stop beside the pool with floodlight in hand and turn full circle, trying to see the entire chamber—a futile attempt, because I'm deep in a forest of glistening gypsum columns, and everywhere I see reflections of my light.

This is why I love caving. I am overwhelmed. The place humbles me.

The chamber feels aware, even more strongly today, if that's possible. I force myself to go to work. I set up a remote flash high on the breakdown pile, aimed upstream. I return to the pool to make the shots. The angle of the light provides good reflections and shadows, and the pictures look great.

I look around, thinking about how to shoot the pool itself. Fifty feet upstream, the water divides around a large flat-topped flowstone that looks perfect as a shooting location. I climb the breakdown to re-aim the remote flash—now it will light the pool from the side. Then I make my way upstream and step over to the flowstone. The view is exquisite, the side lighting dramatic.

The first shots suffer from hot spots from my helmet light. I swivel it toward the ceiling and reshoot; the results are exactly what I want.

When I reach up to return my helmet light to horizontal, I accidentally turn it off.

I HAVE ALWAYS LOVED the utter darkness of caves. I once guided a group of three autistic children into a cave in Virginia, a place with its own beauty and presence. The children were nervous and fidgety, but when I turned out the light they fell silent for so long that their teacher became concerned. When he asked, "Everybody all right?" I heard only satisfied murmurs. I turned on a dim light, aimed away from the group to avoid startling anyone. The kids were relaxed and happy, blissfully absorbing the darkness. The teacher told me later that he had never seen them so peaceful. Autistic children are extremely sensitive to disturbing noises and lights. The cool darkness of a cave was exactly what those kids needed.

The ceremonial chamber points out the irony of cave photography. To take pictures we must use light, but bathing a perpetually dark place in light robs it of its essence. Does it know? Could it resent artificial light? I've been caving since I was a boy, and that question has never before occurred to me.

In darkness the stream sounds louder, almost alive, a voice that ebbs and swells. The original tenants must have heard that. A feeling of peace creeps over me, and I realize how tired I am. I sit beside my tripod, lie back on my pack, and close my eyes to better listen to the stream.

The feeling of someone with me is overwhelming.

I stand in the ceremonial chamber, which is dimly lit by a glow that seems to come from the stream. A young woman and her daughter of eleven or twelve stand near me on the same flowstone, looking downward as they talk to each other. They are not aware of me.

The woman is beautiful, with olive skin, dark curly hair, and dark eyes. The girl has the same hair and eyes but lighter skin. They wear leather clothes and look robust and healthy—and very much alike.

The original inhabitants of this cave, shown to me by the power of the ceremonial chamber!

Then the daughter raises her head and looks directly at me.

I am taken aback. The girl seems curious, open, and unafraid of me. We look at each other for a long moment and both smile. The mother still does not see me, but she senses something and is wary and concerned. She would disapprove.

I understand that the girl's name is Alice and that I am in her chosen place.

I wake slowly. I had not been aware of sleeping, and the dream was so vivid that I believed I was living it. I slept half an hour, and during that time I spanned thousands of years.

Over dinner, I relate the experience to Roger and Mira. They raise their eyebrows, but not in scorn. We all know that what happened in the ceremonial chamber yesterday is beyond explanation—beyond even the spookiest cave experiences we have shared in the past. Even so, Roger and Mira resist acknowledging that I made contact with one of the cave's original inhabitants.

I SLEEP RESTLESSLY, but when I see how Roger looks in the morning I consider myself lucky to have slept at all. He had a vivid dream of the ceremonial chamber—a group of people around a fire, someone singing. He didn't sleep afterward. Roger is a geological engineer, not given to flights of fancy. I remind him that my great-aunt and great-uncle told of lifelong cave dreams after a single visit here. He no longer raises his eyebrows about my dream.

Our flight home leaves tomorrow afternoon; we must leave here at midday today. Mira spends the morning finishing her preliminary inventory and collecting paint chips from the floor below the paintings, for carbon dating. Roger and I survey the entrance chamber and begin the survey of the living chamber.

We are out of the cave by one o'clock and do hard physical work for the rest of the day. We pack up and move everything to the rappel rope—two loads for each of us. I climb first; Roger follows. Mira attaches the loads one by one, and Roger and I haul them up. Then Mira climbs out and we begin carrying the gear to the car. We are on the terrible road by six. The trip downhill is truly scary.

We find a small hotel beside the river, where we are the only guests. After dinner we talk over wine. "These people were almost surely animist believers," Mira says. "They felt the spirit of every person and place and animal. They believed they left their imprint on the places they loved."

I think of the copper, the growing grain, and the paintings. "They were impressive people."

"That's an impressive chamber," she says.

MOTHER AND I never use torches in the spirit chamber—the stream sound guides us—but when we go together, we hold hands to avoid stumbling over each other. Today as we enter the chamber I again sense someone else, and Mother squeezes my hand. She feels it too, which doesn't surprise me.

I still don't understand. Does the spirit remember someone from an earlier time?

Mother stops in her spot, and I walk upstream toward my own place and lie down. The feeling of another presence is very strong. I am curious and not worried, for the spirit would never lead me to harm.

As I drift toward sleep I remember Mother telling me that when she first met Father, he could hear the stream flowing to the sea. I hear that now, and the sound draws me out of myself.

Mother and I are together in my spot. I can see her, because the stream glows, as it sometimes does in my dreams. The feeling of someone else nearby is so strong that I look up. I am astounded to see a man watching me, a stranger. He sees me! His eyes twinkle as we look at each other, and we both smile.

I know he's not truly here with me. We can see each other because the spirit remembers him from some other time.

I wake alarmed, not quite afraid. Mother comes instantly when I call her.

"I saw a man. He was right here. He looked friendly. He knew I was here and smiled at me."

"You dreamed this?" Mother sounds worried.

"A dream of seeing, like yours." Everyone knows about Mother's dreams. When our boat burned at Rivermouth, she learned of it by dreaming. I also know the rest of the story, that it was my grandfather who burned the boat, Father's father. Nobody told me that. I figured it out from Mother's paintings.

Mother's concern makes me think. Could what I do in the spirit chamber invite enemies into our midst? I see immediately that it could not. If I know the spirit best, I will have to be my own guide, with the help of the spirit, who never lies.

"Mother, the man was not a threat. He wanted to be my friend."

She shakes her head. "You know the spirit best, Alys. Trust yourself, but tell me if you have more dreams like that one."

We walk outside into a warm summer evening. Later, I lie awake listening to insects sing and thinking of the man I saw. The spirit made that happen. Why? Will I see him again? Perhaps we have something to do together.

Being the one who knows the spirit best is sometimes a burden.

THE MAN IN THE SPIRIT CHAMBER is still on my mind when I wake, but life on the Benchland goes on as usual. Aunt Angela and Aunt Ragna are both pregnant this summer, and when she's pregnant, Aunt Angela is even more short-tempered than usual. Uncle Aramel and Aunt Inge's daughter Eydis are in love and want to marry, which would make her my aunt too. Fedr is building a third hearth in the sleeping chamber, because last winter our two hearths were so crowded.

Eydis's younger brother Kyle is also an accomplished builder. He and Uncle Aramel have learned for years from Fedr. Last winter Kyle was very sick. He has always been my special friend, and I was horrified to learn in the spirit chamber that he might die. Mother and Aunt Inge treated him every day, and I was grateful and relieved when he recovered, although he still looks thin and pale. I realized then that I wanted him to be more than a friend—that I hoped we might marry someday, even though he's seven years older. Of course I haven't told anyone how I feel, especially Kyle, but I don't think knowing would surprise him.

Fedr and Kyle and Uncle Aramel would like to build a few houses below us, close to the river, because we are already 35 people and will soon outgrow the cave. Then we will need a real village that can expand.

Uncle Sigurd doesn't like the idea of any of us living down by the river. His warrior days are over, but he has always felt that the bench is the best place for us because it is secure against attack. Uncle Sigurd grew up in a time of war against raiders and fought many battles. He was a big part of ending the raids, but to him the threat hasn't ended. "We live where we do for a reason," he says.

Uncle Sigurd's concern is not the only problem with living near the river. I also worry about living too far from the spirit chamber to go there every day, and Mother feels the same. What will I do if Kyle builds a house and wants to move?

KYLE'S OLDER BROTHER LEIF, Uncle Druian, Uncle Geyr, and Father are our most active and successful hunters. They left yesterday on a trip of several days. Grandfather and Uncle Sigurd don't go hunting as often as when I was younger. Grandfather is upset that he can't climb as well as he could, but he and Uncle Sigurd still spend every day at their work area. Also, Grandfather has more time for me than before. He made me a beautiful bracelet of redmetal, and I love it and wear it all the time.

My two grandmothers and Aunt Inge work daily in the garden. Today they are cross because the puppies ran through the garden and dug holes. What bad dogs! They are too big now to be running so wild. Uncle Geyr and Father brought them from Rivermouth after a trading trip in the spring. They were wiggly furballs then, two months old, but now they are much bigger. Our old dog Star snaps and snarls at them to make them behave, and they fear her—but nothing else. Star still tends the small children and keeps them from wandering. Someday the puppies will be useful, but for now they're funny and destructive. Both are girls. Otherwise we would be overwhelmed by puppies.

Grandmother Quitana is teaching me to make clay pots. My pots are crude compared to hers, but Mother says they are better than any pot she ever made. I love painting my pots. One has a painting of the puppies curled up in a ball. Grandfather baked that pot for me, and it works well even if it is crooked.

I am learning the prayer songs from Mother and Aunt Inge, and when I come of age I will start helping

Mother with our ceremonies. Mother has Aunt Inge for a teacher, but I have them both. It seems strange to me that these wise women who know so much think I know more of the spirit than they. I am grateful to them for teaching me.

Today the spirit chamber feels empty, but I think of the man from my dream. I feel sure I will learn something important from him.

MY DREAMS are making me crazy.

I'm back at work, but my heart isn't in it. Two days ago I returned from a trip to Mexico, where I photographed a weeklong expedition into one of the world's deepest caves. The cave was spectacular, and the photography was a complete success, but I rushed back so I could continue work on the pictures of the cave paintings from Sweden.

I said the ceremonial chamber had a presence that reminded me of the sacred cenotes in the Yucatan, but I take that back. The cenotes feel eerie because they contain human artifacts—shards of pots tossed in as offerings, and occasionally a skull—but they are not a patch on the ceremonial chamber in Alice's Cave, as we've named it. The people who lived there left a magical imprint that I can feel.

The cenotes feel like tombs. The ceremonial chamber feels inhabited.

On the long flight westward over the Atlantic, we talked at length about my dream and Roger's. Mira laughed and said we were suffering from job stress, but that was then. Now she has dreams too. Roger and Mira haven't met Alice in person, as I have, if only once, but we all dream regularly of the cave—mostly the ceremonial chamber, but also the living chamber, including its people. Mira dreamed of a woman painting its back wall. I am collecting our emails describing the dreams.

After we relinquish the cave to the tender mercies of the Swedish Ministry of Culture, we will publish everything we know about it, with photographs. Meanwhile we will keep the entire affair to ourselves.

WE MEET FOR DINNER after my Mexico trip, two weeks after we return from Sweden. We discuss our dreams and our considered reflections about our experience in the cave. Mira has the carbon-dating results: the paint chips are 5,200 years old, give or take a hundred years. We agree we must return, because we feel an obligation to document the cave. We have obligations to ourselves as well; the dreams have become a significant part of our lives.

This will be our longest cave expedition. Mira will document the living chamber, and that alone is a big project—she can't estimate how big, because she has seen only the topmost layer, but she will need several weeks at least. Roger and I will survey the cave, and I will photograph every chamber and passage, as well as the shelf. We will have no trouble keeping busy while Mira works, and all the while the cave itself will surely interfere by inducing dreams.

The realtor in Rivermouth says the quarry closes down for the year in September. Once the snow falls, the only way out will be by helicopter. We're already into May. We can't possibly spend the winter in the cave, and nobody wants to put the trip off until next spring. Mira wouldn't be able to go then at all; next summer she will lead a seminar—ironically, on properly documenting artifacts in ancient settlements.

We know we should be packing rather than talking. We'll leave as soon as possible and hope we can finish without being trapped by snow.

With that decision behind us, we set to work.

ALL THREE OF US have jobs, so leaving for the summer requires arrangements. For Mira, this is no problem—she's on sabbatical leave this year and has been working alone. That's why she could go in April. Roger's request for a leave of absence is quickly granted. My work is an issue; I have several jobs on my summer calendar and must find substitutes—not simple, because my reputation will be on the line every time. Over the next week, I exchange email and phone calls with clients and potential subs. They are all curious, and that makes me nervous. Eventually my journalist friends will smell a story, and for this story, any one of them would sell us out in a heartbeat. I hate elaborate lies, so I simply say I've developed an unexpected conflict.

I must also deal with my condo. There is no one in my life to miss me—I don't even have a cat to come home to—but the apartment should not remain empty the whole summer. This problem solves itself when I mention it to Mira: a Polish colleague is seeking a temporary place to live. Roger and Mira's own house is no problem. Their place tends itself while they are away, because they rent rooms to students.

Planning in earnest quickly restores me to my normal self, fully engaged in what I'm doing. My feelings of vagueness and dissatisfaction are replaced by an urgent need to return to Alice's Cave.

Roger and Mira are also eager. Mira envisions a book from this project—the definitive monograph on the most stunning assemblage of late Neolithic artifacts and paintings found in decades. I see a seventy-five dollar coffee-table book with full-page photographs. Roger, who has never been able to pass up an opportunity to explore a cave, also wants to document the local geology, with an eye to finding other caves in the area.

THE PLANNING is complex. We'll need a ton of equipment and food. We'll have satellite phone service for medical emergencies, but we won't be able to run to the market if we forget something. What we don't ship, we will buy in Stockholm when we arrive; we certainly don't want to make buying trips into Rivermouth. People would wonder what we're about, and we don't want news of the cave to get out yet. The Swedish government could always shut the cave down and stop our work, whether or not I own the land.

We must have a truck with four-wheel drive, big enough to haul all our gear and rugged enough to carry us up that pig trail of a road and take us off-road to the mountaintop. We don't want to lug everything from the road, as we did in April.

Consider batteries. Our laptops, cameras, lights, and phones have them. They will need charging, and our brief inspection revealed no electrical outlets in the cave. I buy two solar panels that unfold to the size of pillow cases. For the helmet lights we bring a bale of double-A batteries plus rechargeables in case we run out. This topic is only one of many. Don't get me started on toilet paper, plastic bags, antibiotics, duct tape, spare cards for the cameras, and portable hard disks. Most cave expeditions don't last more than ten days. This one is far beyond the limits of our experience, and we can only hope we don't make crippling mistakes.

For ten frantic days we live and work in my condo, buying supplies and packing them, accumulating a mountain of goods in my living room. As we work we ask ourselves questions. How did the people who lived in Alice's Cave reach the shelf? Through some other entrance to the cave? Or did they climb? Either upward or downward, climbing would have involved a daunting amount of vertical. They must have been in good physical shape. What did they eat? What were their family lives like? How did they spend their days? Alice looked happy and healthy. Weak people couldn't have survived.

On the first of June the van from SAS Cargo Services picks up our eight crates of gear, and five hours later we are airborne.

"Dr. Kramnick, please."

"I'm sorry, she's on sabbatical."

"Well, actually, I was trying to reach Jarrett Eriksson, for a cave photo project. His phone message says he's unavailable this summer, and out of contact. I had hoped I could find him through her. I wasn't able to reach her at home."

"I'm sorry, but I can't help you. Perhaps you could try to reach her husband."

"I did. I found out he's on leave of absence. Please, if you hear from her, ask her to get in touch with Joel Harte."

Roger and Mira and Jarrett, all AWOL? There is only one possible explanation. They're in a cave somewhere, and they don't want anyone to know about it. Not even me. Perhaps especially me. But I'll find them.

Jarrett and I were journalism students together. He already had a masters in geology when he had an epiphany that convinced him he wanted to work as a cave journalist. After we graduated, we worked together often, but then he got into photography. He has become the premier cave photographer. I see his pictures everywhere, and they regularly win awards.

I love caving, and for my living I go on trips and then write articles about them. Jarrett and I haven't worked together much recently, but five years ago we did a Lechuguilla restoration and cleanup trip, three weeks underground in the most beautiful cave in the universe, and our book with my writing and his pictures made money for both of us.

Now he's off somewhere in a cave without me! For shame, Jarrett. You should have told me.

I BEGIN by searching the recent news for his name, but to no avail. I search the archives of all the caving journals. I find no word of Jarrett's doings anywhere.

I don't quit easily, so I hire a private investigator to find him. I have results in three days. Jarrett recently inherited a big piece of land somewhere in Sweden, about which I know only one thing: it's my next destination.

OUR FIRST BIG PROBLEM is the truck. The two I arranged to test-drive both lack four-wheel drive, the result of a telephone language barrier, so we spend two full days staying in a Stockholm tourist hotel while we look at trucks. Our gear remains in storage with SAS Cargo. Eventually we find an ancient Dodge diesel pickup with four-wheel drive—big cab with four doors, and enough room in back for all our stuff. It will be perfect if only it will get us where we want to go before its service life ends. It was a fire truck at one point, and I have always wanted a red car.

We don't need to buy much in Stockholm except our small supply of fresh meat and produce—for most of the trip we will survive on canned food and freeze-dried caver chow. We do have to buy butane. We will cook over butane to avoid wood fires; we need an enormous number of butane canisters and clean out several large outdoor stores.

We will camp outside, reserving the right to move into the entry chamber in bad weather. Mira doesn't like that, but sleeping in the rain appeals to her even less. She defends the outdoors as zealously as the cave. Originally I wanted to bring seeds and plant a small garden—if the original people could do it, we could too—but Mira vetoed the idea, pointing out that many of the paintings show outdoor activity and anything we do outside is likely to disrupt ancient artifacts.

THE TRUCK RATTLES INTO RIVERMOUTH on the seventh of June. The day is young, and the place is beautiful, with morning sun coming over the sea. We're well rested after a night in a fairly good hotel one hour south on the coast. We buy diesel fuel and start up the river.

The canyon is gorgeous in its summer finery, with blooms of every color along the river and roadside. The road has almost no traffic, but the hotel-restaurant businesses we see every few miles seem to have guests. Cattle graze beside the river, and the flocks of sheep have fresh crops of tiny lambs.

The river and road climb through a spectacular steep canyon, with roaring whitewater and deep road cuts. Then, in one of those mountain surprises, the river canyon opens into a green flower-strewn valley, and above us looms the shelf.

It is almost noon when we stop beside the river, below the place where we will live for weeks. The quarry operation is busy, with dump trucks moving around on their inner road, but my eye is drawn higher, to the dramatic cliff, essentially vertical, that makes up the top half of the wall above the quarry. Nearer the bottom, the slope softens—no longer vertical, but still steep as it plunges to river level.

We stopped in this same place in April, but I now recognize the cliff face as an old friend. One of the most dramatic painted scenes in the cave shows a bloody battle on this cliff. I've studied my photo of that painting, and I can't help visualizing the battle now. Three defenders stand at the top of the steep slope fighting off a group of perhaps a dozen men who are attacking from below. Several bloody bodies lie at the bottom of the slope.

When I sent my photos of the battle scene to Mira, she called me within the hour. "Do you remember? I couldn't understand why the original people would choose a cave, when many contemporaries lived in villages. This picture explains it all. Late Neolithic villages were sometimes reduced to mass graves by raiding enemies. I think those people chose to live in Alice's Cave because it was easy to defend. *Look* at that cliff!"

THE TRUCK FAR OUTPERFORMS our April rental car on the terrible road, and we don't have to hike, because we drive off-road over the rocks and hillocks all the way to the ridgetop. We see our rigging tree from the April trip but drive a mile and a quarter beyond it, closer to the cave entrance. When we look over the edge, however, our view down is blocked by a long outcrop that will interfere with hauling loads up and down. We move a hundred feet farther south, beyond the end of the outcrop, to rig the descent. Roger and I unload the gear and then move the truck to the trees and tarp it in camo.

We are higher on the mountain than we were in April, and I rig 500 feet of rope. Mira straps on a rappel harness and disappears over the edge. Three minutes later the radio squawks, "Off rope." She landed without difficulty, well south of the cave.

The crates weigh about a hundred pounds each. We have a cargo net, the remnant of a cargo drop on some long-forgotten trip. It is big enough for a single crate. This is a simple drop, quite vertical, and the net glides to the ground beside Mira eight times out of eight.

Our rigging will stay on the cliff. If anything happens to it we will rappel down to the quarry, apologize and explain, and hike to the truck.

We set up camp where we did before, near where the stream emerges from the breakdown. We leave as much gear as possible at the bottom of the rappel rope but still have plenty to carry. We aren't completely installed in camp until nine o'clock—still broad daylight. Sunset will be about 10:30 tonight, but we won't see it. Our camp looks forty miles east, to the shore, but only about a hundred feet west. Alice lived her life without seeing many sunsets.

We have food for a few days of luxury eating before it's all cave fare all the time. Tonight we have steaks grilled with mushrooms, corn, and beer. To our astonishment, dinner includes a treat—a northern lights show before the moon rises. Not the finest display we've seen—the three of us have done ice caves in Greenland—but unexpected and beautiful, a fine omen for the beginning of this trip.

OUR FIRST JOB is to enlarge the entry. We'll need to carry a great deal of gear into the cave, too much for our original scant crawlway. This means a full day's hard labor for Roger and me. The entryway grows as we work, and Mira is in and out of the cave a dozen times, getting ready for her first real workday tomorrow.

At some point, sweaty and tired, Roger remarks that one small blast would make our work much easier, if only we had the gear. Mira hears him. "Roger Kramnick," she says, in her most dangerous tone, "if you—" and then hesitates, unable to find a sufficiently dire threat in English. She finally mutters something in Polish, gives him a killing look, and disappears into the cave. We won't be blasting.

At day's end we have a walking passage through the breakdown. Its floor is a few feet higher than ground level, so we must climb to reach it from either side, but not much, and to make that easier we place large stepping stones. Roger and I are happy the job is done—this is the hardest physical work of the trip—and all of us are pleased with the result.

After dinner we take our beer and pay a short social call on the living chamber, where we stand gawking like tourists. The place is exactly as we left it, with its eerie sense of suspended life. The hearths and paintings are as familiar as old friends. The ceremonial chamber calls to me, but we're not suited up, and I don't have knee pads. And I would never go there with a bottle of beer in hand.

MIRA'S MAJOR TASK on this trip is documenting the human artifacts in the living chamber. Roger and I will survey the cave. It will be a relief to escape Mira's red lines. We must still be careful—every step we take will add our skin oils, dandruff, cast-off hairs, and lint to the cave—but untrodden passage feels better than a red-tape walkway.

We begin our survey with the ceremonial chamber, to stay out of Mira's way. We establish our first station at the top of the breakdown pile where we enter. From there we work our way to the west end of the room, a little at a time. Sightlines are limited to less than a hundred feet, because from wall to wall and end to end the chamber is a forest of tall stalagmites. The entire room is heavily decorated, and kaleidoscopic reflections of our lights gleam everywhere.

From our first station to the west end of the room is 270 feet, more than we had guessed. The stream emerges from a fissure in the rock there, and a walking-height passage leads further west into the seductive unknown. Today we're surveying, not exploring. We look into the westward lead and then turn regretfully back to our job.

The stream makes the ceremonial chamber and living chamber feel like the cave's main trunk. When we follow that westward passage we may get a better feel for the overall layout, but we already know the cave is not simple. Along the ceremonial chamber's south wall are several upward-sloping leads and a low open crawl that leads to another large, highly-decorated chamber. We also see dozens of alcoves that could hide more leads.

The ceremonial chamber is shaped like an arrowhead. It's about a hundred feet wide at the entry tunnel and half that at the far end, but its size and shape don't even hint at its effect. Alice came here with only a torch for light. That must have been frightening for a young girl who believed that places like this have their own animus. What would give her such courage? She must have felt safe here. This chamber's magic must have been part of her life. Maybe she was born here.

By the end of the day we have established 21 survey stations in the ceremonial chamber, and Roger's sketch pad has the first-ever rough drawing of the room. Days of work remain simply to fill in the details of this one chamber. We are exhausted, and when we emerge into the living chamber we find Mira just as tired. And this is only the first day.

THE NEXT FEW DAYS drain us. When we stop work in early evening we are almost too tired to eat. For Mira, the work is excruciatingly slow. "Every time I pick something up, I see other artifacts below it. All this work will be worthless if I'm not methodical." She photographs every object in place before she examines it and has already filled a notebook with sketches and minute descriptions. She works one small area at a time, sifting dirt and gravel through screen to find even the smallest objects. It is already obvious that this room alone is beyond what she can do this summer.

When we finally finish our work in the ceremonial chamber, Roger and I survey our way westward. The passage we saw on the first day leads to a space that is truly cavernous—855 feet long. It is undecorated, walled and roofed with enormous slabs. To our surprise, it has no stream. At its west end we enter a maze of twisty little passages, all alike. Finding our way through is easy enough; a route marked with stacked rocks, undisturbed for five thousand years, leads out of the maze to the bottom of a pit. We decide to survey the maze before climbing the pit, and we find no fewer than four more leads, both upward and downward. This is a big cave. We still have no idea how big.

Inheritance

MIRA HAS ALMOST MANIC ENERGY even though she's exhausted. She complains of sleeping poorly because she can't stop thinking about what she finds—loud thoughts, she says. She hears the murmur of the original people, for whom these artifacts were simply the stuff of their lives, everyday objects. "I feel I can't move quickly enough," she says on one lunch break. "I have to force myself to slow down, or I'll make mistakes. There are so many things here! I feel I must find every one, and that could take years." Mira normally works with almost-clinical detachment. Her desperation worries me.

"Jarrett, I've never seen her so agitated." Roger and I are back in the ceremonial chamber. "She has me a bit freaked. She usually sleeps soundly, but for the last few nights she's been restless enough to keep me awake, and she mutters in her sleep. No wonder I'm tired."

My own problem is dreams. Every night now, always about the ceremonial chamber. Lying awake, I'm tempted to go there by myself. I feel I could sleep soundly there. I might be wrong, but the pull is strong. I find that both fascinating and alarming. I want those dreams, but I fear they could be loosening my grip on reality.

18

LARGE PIECE OF LAND, indeed. The District Property Registry in Stockholm shows the transfer in 2011 of eighteen hundred hectares to Jarrett Eriksson of Baltimore, Maryland, USA. More than four thousand acres. Almost seven square miles. I find a geological map on the net. The area is geologically complex, with some surprising volcanic rock, but much of it is limestone, likely to have caves.

Seven square miles! Jarrett and company could be anywhere.

I buy topo maps from a bookstore; Stockholm still has bookstores with paper maps. I pencil in the boundaries of the property, which is long and narrow. The east boundary is a river, which later flows into the sea at the little town of Rivermouth, where I spend the night in a hotel.

In the morning I drive three hours upriver to the southeast corner of Jarrett's kingdom and then continue slowly north along its eastern edge. On my left is a high limestone ridge, a likely place for caves, but steep and impossible for me to reach. I come to the north boundary of the property without seeing any way to approach the ridge, and I stop to consult my map. The other side of the ridge appears to be less steep. It has a road that eventually meets the coast well south of Rivermouth. I sigh and start back downriver.

The sun is low by the time I find the road, which is gravel. I won't be driving it until tomorrow; for my jet-lagged body, this day is over. I find a small hotel on the coast. After dinner I look at Google Earth for a birds-eye view of Jarrett's property and plan my day tomorrow.

I TURN ONTO THE GRAVEL ROAD early in the morning, but the going is slow, and I don't enter the west side of Jarrett's property until nearly noon.

The high ridge—now on my right—is not the only likely cave terrain; near the northwest corner of the property, the road climbs a crossing ridge that runs westward and could also have caves. The most basic way to locate caves is by ridgewalking. I need to search both ridges. I won't have to walk the east-west ridge, because I find a rough dirt road that follows it until it leaves Jarrett's property.

I drive west on that road, stopping often to look on both sides of the ridge. I see a few caves, but cavers have cars, and I don't see any. The road appears untraveled, and when I reach the west boundary of the property I turn around.

When I get back to the gravel road I turn north, heading toward the highest point of the limestone ridge east of me. The upper part of the road is awful, and my rental Subaru suffers grievously. It is after four when I emerge from a warren of gullies onto the ridge, which unfortunately does not have a road. Driving off-road is forbidden by my rental contract in a bold-print paragraph I had to initial, so I park the car. I have six hours of light left. I can safely undertake a two-hour hike.

I reach the backbone of the ridge by 5:30 and look down at the river road I drove yesterday morning. The drop to the river isn't sheer; a substantial shelf of land lies below me, part way down. It looks inaccessible.

I would not be surprised to find caves there. I'm getting close. I can feel it.

I walk south along the ridgetop, admiring the view eastward over the hills to the sea and keeping my eye on the shelf below me. It's after six now—past my turnaround time—but the trek back to the car will be easy, and I still have lots of light. I decide to hike until seven.

The search pays off at 6:45, when I find a truck parked in a group of trees and tarped in camo, a Jarrett trademark. Five minutes later I find his rappel rope. I can see their camp on the shelf below—two tents and a large collection of gear. No people. They're in the cave, of course.

Now I have to decide when to drop in on them. It can't be tonight, because my gear is all back at the car. I don't have to return to the hotel; I can camp at the car and return here first thing tomorrow morning with my gear—and the steaks and beer. I brought them as an apology for crashing the party. I *knew* I would need them.

See you in the morning, Jarrett.

19

TWO MONTHS HAVE PASSED since I saw the man in the spirit chamber, but I think about him every day when I go there. That worries Mother and Aunt Inge. I understand, but I trust the spirit.

This morning I talk to Father about it. He is the only man who knows the spirit chamber well, and he and Mother are together because of the spirit. He doesn't share her worry. "Alys, you were born to know the spirit chamber. Things will happen to you there that nobody else will understand. You must judge for yourself." Father hugs me the way only he does, and I know again why I love him.

I come to the spirit chamber, and the moment I enter I know the man is back. I head straight for my own place, where I saw him before.

I am full of questions about him. Why can I see him? Why does it feel so important? And why does he appear on a day when I've thought so much about him? The spirit offers no explanations.

Could it be that the man is important to our future?

I'm so agitated that drifting into sleep takes much longer than usual.

He sits across from me, by the hearth, but a brilliant light comes from his head and blinds me. When I hold up my hand to shield my eyes, he reaches to his head and the light disappears, but I still see colored spots. I have never seen such a light, except from the sun.

He is embarrassed about the light. When my eyes begin to recover, I smile, and his face relaxes.

He smiles, and I understand that he knows my name.

I still see stars and blobs of light when I wake. He remembers me! He knows my name!

"IT LOOKED LIKE THE SUN shining from his head." I am talking with Grandmother Quitana as she makes a pot near the outdoor work area. I am painting a pot I made earlier. It was baked in the oven two days ago and did not crack. I'm always happy to have another surface to paint.

"Have you told your mother, and Inge?"

"Not yet. Mother is already concerned."

Grandmother nods and silently watches me work. "Alys, your pictures are beautiful. You should paint what you see in your dreams."

"I wish I could paint my dreams on the walls, but by the time I am of age there will be no more room. Mother's and Aunt Ragna's paintings cover more of the wall every year. And painting pots is difficult. I make mistakes because I can't see the whole painting at once."

I have made a fine brush of hemp fiber, and as we talk I paint a picture of Aunt Angela, who is beautiful when she is pregnant. But I want to paint a picture of the man with the light on his head. On a flat surface, not a curved pot.

"Why don't you make square pots?" Grandmother always has good ideas. "You could even paint on flat clay slabs."

The answer to my old worry! Flat clay slabs, thin ones! Why didn't I think of it? I would never run out of space for my paintings, because I could always make more slabs!

Grandmother laughs. "Even when you were tiny, your eyes sparkled when you were pleased. Let's make a slab for you." She is working her pot on a thick piece of shale. We have plenty of those. I tried painting pictures on them, but eventually they all broke apart, and the paintings I made that way are lost. Grandmother sets her pot aside. We wet the shale, put down a lump of clay, and flatten it into a slab as thick as my thumb. A clay slab! It is three handspans long and two wide—my hands, not Grandmother's. I smooth the top with one of Grandmother's wooden tools. Tomorrow, after the clay dries, I will carefully lift it off the shale by using one of Grandfather's thin slate wedges. Then he will bake it for me. If it doesn't break, I will paint it.

I try to thank Grandmother, but talking is hard when you're crying.

Mother promised we would find a place for me to paint my story. Father thought I would find the answer in the spirit chamber, but it came almost accidentally, from my wise grandmother. Of course it is no accident. It comes from the spirit, and from the man with sunlight shining from his head.

I know exactly what I will paint first.

I DIDN'T SLEEP at all last night, and by dinnertime today I was dizzy and stumbling. Even so, tonight I lie awake in my bag for hours—until I finally give in. I get up, trying not to disturb Roger and Mira, who are also exhausted and seem to be asleep, judging by the sounds. I suit up in moonlight and don't need my helmet light until I'm nearly at the cave entrance. The rising moon is framed in our enlarged entryway, which has increased the light level in the entry cavern during the day as well.

In the living chamber, the outdoor chill gives way to the cave's usual moist comfort—55 degrees and 95 percent humidity. How nice that change must have been for people who lived here in the winter.

I have no cameras—only a utility blanket. I'm here for sleep, not work.

As I enter the ceremonial chamber I know immediately that coming here was a good idea. I climb down to a level space beside the pool, spread out my

blanket next to the old hearth, and lie down to listen—
and sleep, I hope.

Within minutes I am more relaxed than I have been
for days. The sound of the stream fills my ears and
suggests images of this place in other times.

> *Alice sits facing me. She looks startled and
> throws her hand up before her eyes. I am
> embarrassed to realize that my helmet light is
> still on. I quickly switch it off, but she is reeling
> from five watts of LED light. I seek desperately
> for some way to help her, but she recovers quickly
> and gives me a shy smile. I am overwhelmed with
> relief.*

I wake after only a few minutes, exhausted but
exhilarated because I have again closed the gap
between me and Alice. I am eager to know what comes
next, but my most immediate need comes first: a full
night of sleep.

WHEN I CHECK MY WATCH, I'm shocked to see that half
the morning is gone. I stumble to my feet, grab my
blanket, and make my way out to the living chamber,
where I almost collide with Roger. He looks well rested
for the first time since we arrived.

"Jarrett, you spent the night in the ceremonial
chamber?"

"A desperate attempt to get some sleep."

"Mira and I slept well, for a change, with no dreams. She's making breakfast. I came to find you. Did you encounter your dream friends?"

"The girl, not the mother, and only briefly. I felt stupid because my light blinded her."

"Tell us about it while we eat."

Outside, I sit on a rock to remove my gear. As I stand to carry everything to the tent, my eye falls on the rappel rope. Even from a distance, I can see that it's swaying. Roger follows my gaze upward, and we both see a figure back off the cliff above and begin the rappel down our rope.

"Who the hell is that?" I sound as shocked as I feel.

Who could have found us? And so soon! Did we inadvertently leave a trail? It's clearly a caver, with a lot of rappel experience. A large caving pack hangs below him.

Roger and I walk toward the rappel rope. Mira joins us, also looking upward.

"Oh, God," I say. "It's Joel Harte."

"OFF ROPE," Joel says sweetly, as he unclips. "Hello Jarrett, Roger, Mira. You forgot to send my invitation." He picks up his pack and starts toward the tents.

"Joel, I would be lying if I said you were welcome." I put as much acid into my tone as possible and try unsuccessfully to head him off. "You presume on our friendship. What do you want?"

"You know what I want. I want the story."

"Four words, Joel. None of your business."

"People always have reasons for secrecy, Jarrett. I don't know yours yet, but I will."

We arrive at the tents, and in one glance he takes in Mira's trove of notebooks, sample bags, portable cameras, and voice recorders. "Would we be indulging in a little undercover archaeology, then? It's that simple?"

"You can't have the story, Joel. It would kill the project."

"Give it to me for later, then. You can't get away with hoarding ancient treasures."

"We don't want to get away with anything. We're documenting evidence of human habitation of a cave, which we're fully qualified to do. We intend to turn over the documentation and the cave to the Swedish government. We need a year."

Mira and Roger flinch. A year?

"A year for me is forever. I could be dead in a year. I want a story, and not a year from now. You can't stay here beyond the summer in any case. It gets cold, they tell me. I'll leave you alone for four months. Then I get exclusive newspaper and magazine rights. I want to write the book, with your photographs in it. Mira, I'm not concerned about the book you must be planning. You can have whatever academic credit comes out of this."

"No." By now I'm really angry. "Not negotiable. Once this cave is known it will be gone forever, because the Swedish government will close it."

"You have no choice. If you don't agree, what you're doing will be in next week's news."

"Intending to wire it from here, are you?" Joel and I are right in each other's faces.

Roger steps between us. "Let me suggest a truce. Let's eat. We haven't had breakfast, and we have a fine selection of cans and freeze dry. After that, perhaps we can show Joel what we're doing and explain the problem."

As always, Roger's calm is contagious. I'm sorry Joel is here, but my flush of anger feels childish. We don't have time for drama.

"Here." Joel puts down his pack. "If you put the beer in the stream now, it will chill in time for dinner. You'll find it under the steaks." He extends his hand to me, and I shake it, reluctantly.

BREAKFAST IS A TENSE AFFAIR. I spend the time kicking myself for not constructing a better roadblock to keep people like Joel out of this place. How did he find us? I won't give him the satisfaction of asking. Soon enough his ego will drive him to brag about his clever detective work.

I'm sorry to see he has come prepared for caving, with suit, helmet, and even booties and gloves. Joel is an arrogant jerk, and my stomach lurched when Roger suggested showing him the cave, but as matters stand that's inevitable. Also, Joel and I have worked together on cave books, and I can't imagine a writer better suited to this project.

Still, I'll never agree to any deadline. The truth is that I don't want anyone to know about the cave. Ever. It's *my* cave! It's on my property, and I should make the rules. I don't need a lecture about public trusts or national treasures. I know all that, but to me this is far more than a cave project. I've made contact with someone from thousands of years ago!

I think of Alice, smiling after being stunned by my light. How could anyone else understand? Even Roger and Mira? How can I explain, without appearing to be ready for a straitjacket?

BEFORE WE CAN OPEN UP to Joel, he and I have business to conduct. I handwrite a non-disclosure agreement in which he promises to keep confidential everything he knows about the cave and our project, and we agree to allow him publication rights, with details to be negotiated. No time frame is mentioned. If we never agree to a date, Joel is permanently bound to silence.

He bridles. "What if we can't agree? I'm out in the cold?"

"Joel—" I begin, and then pause. My anger has subsided to a cold distaste. "Because we have worked together, I will give you this one chance to publish the cave story of your lifetime. This cave is unlike anything you or I have ever known. You'll see—if you sign. I'll be reasonable about the final agreement, except that I will never agree to four months or any other hard deadline. So far we know only the first layer of the story, and once the cave is gone it will be gone forever. I won't change a word on this paper. You can take it or leave it. But if you leave it and wreck this project, your career will be over. If you hurt me I will tell, and you know how cavers feel about informers. So sign or leave."

Roger and Mira look horrified, wishing they were somewhere else.

Joel glares at me, outraged. He thought he held all the cards. He wants to tear up the agreement, throw the shreds in my face, and give me a final piece of his mind on his way up the rope. But he is a caver first, and he senses that I'm right. So the cave wins. Joel signs and hands the paper to Roger and Mira as witnesses.

I will give him this: once he makes up his mind, he drops the attitude. Now he wants to see what we're hiding, and we can put it off no longer.

THE FOUR OF US SUIT UP and head into the cave. Mira knows that Joel is aware of protocol but still lectures him about the red tape paths and not touching—her way of scolding him for intruding.

Joel can't hide being impressed with the living chamber, and as I watch his reaction I see the room through his eyes. We've all been in many caves, but

none of us has ever seen anything like these paintings—
generations of pictorial history covering every wall of
the living chamber. A family diary of an entire colony,
recorded the only available way.

Joel says only, "Whoa!" He stands in the middle of
the huge chamber, turning slowly as he shines his light
all the way around the room. He may be a jerk, but he
appreciates the spectacular.

I am of a mind to end the tour here and march Joel
back out of the cave, but already he is starting down the
red tape path toward the ceremonial chamber. My anger
returns afresh, but trying to head him off will only whet
his interest, so I hold my tongue, and Mira leads us up
into the passage.

Joel might simply be smitten by the beauty of the
place, so different from the living chamber. And
because the ceremonial chamber has no artifacts or
paintings, maybe he'll decide the living chamber is
more interesting.

Wishful thinking, of course. Joel doesn't say
anything when he first sees the room, but his eyebrows
arch into a look of questioning astonishment. Roger,
Mira and I silently agree to say nothing about our own
experiences, but Joel doesn't need prompting. The
presence in the ceremonial chamber is impossible to
ignore. It's enough to rattle even the most pragmatic,
stolid person. Joel doesn't have years of scientific
training to inoculate him against the occult. He is a

caver and something of an artist. For Alice's temple, he will be a pushover.

JOEL'S STEAKS ARE GOOD, and we sit up talking long past the ten o'clock sunset. Joel knows something about Neolithic technology, and we talk at length about copper, pottery, dyes, hemp, grain, and the other advances of Alice's people. Mira takes him back into the entry chamber to show him the details of the smelting oven. We talk about how the group lived—in the cave for the winter, out on the shelf otherwise, secure against attack. We talk about the quarry at the bottom of the hill, which works the same copper source Alice's people used.

Joel looks at Mira. "You won't finish the living chamber this season. Or maybe even next season."

"No, but I could do enough in two long trips that we could turn the cave over to the government in good conscience."

"I suppose I could wait that long."

Most unlike Joel. I am impressed and even grateful.

It's late, and we're all tired. Joel finally broaches the subject we've been expecting. "Tell me about the ceremonial chamber. What's up in there?"

Roger and Mira and I look at each other, trying to decide what to say. Finally Mira answers.

"You'll find out."

Inheritance

21

IF MY OWN ELEVEN-YEAR-OLD DAUGHTER were facing adulthood, marriage, and motherhood within the next few years, I would live in fear of the awful things that could happen to her. But I wouldn't worry if she followed where the spirit led.

I do not know proper words to tell about the spirit of this place. It is with me all the time and has been since I first remember. It guides me and shows me truth. When I'm sick or hurt, it heals me, and it comforts me when babies die. When I'm afraid, I don't have to face my fear alone. I will leave my mark on the spirit chamber, and others will feel me there, as I feel Mother and Aunt Inge—and even Aunt Inge's teacher Yrsa, who died before I was born. We will all be part of the spirit long after we are gone.

Mother grew up with the spirit chamber too. She joined with Father there, so the spirit created me. Why can't she see that meeting the man won't hurt me?

When I leave the spirit chamber, I find her talking with Aunt Inge about it.

"Ana, nothing that comes from the spirit will hurt her." Aunt Inge looks at me with a smile.

"I fear what could happen." Mother hugs me while she answers Aunt Inge over my shoulder. "I want Alys to be able to love and marry and feel the joy of loving her children without being distracted by a man from another time. What if they bond as Olaf and I did? One meeting in the spirit chamber changed my life."

"You bonded with a real person, not a dream. The spirit showed you a truth you already knew in your heart. Even so, I was concerned, because you've always been impulsive. Remember that I warned you exactly as you're warning her, and not very long ago."

"I followed where the spirit led, though, and she will do the same. I wish I knew where that would lead."

Mother's concern worried me at first, but now I see that meeting a person from a different time is the most amazing thing that has ever happened to me—the coming of age of my spirit. That's where my story begins. Everything before was simply to prepare me for the person I will become. Mother and Aunt Inge have always said I know the spirit best. Now I see that's true. I still wish I could have seen the light from the stream when Mother and Father were married, but what is happening to me now is the greatest spirit experience of all.

I struggle to find reassuring words. "Mother, I know this from the spirit. That man and I have something important to do. I will not know him long. Afterward I will return to living my life. But right now I cannot turn away from him."

I AM EXCITED about my clay slabs. I made three, and yesterday Grandfather baked them. Two cracked, but I have my first one to paint! They're much easier to make than pots, and we have plenty of clay, so I can make as many as I want. I will probably paint pictures on slabs all my life. Perhaps hundreds of them, and that worries me, because people could see them in the wrong order. I love to walk around the sleeping chamber looking at the pictures, because they show our life as it happened. If my clay slabs are out of order, they won't tell my story properly.

Potmaking is something I have always done with Grandmother Quitana. I like talking with her while I paint pots. The idea of clay slabs came from one of those talks. Today I ask her about keeping the slabs in order.

"You could do it the same way I keep track of days. I make a mark every day, and circle every five marks. I start a new count every month." We go into the sleeping chamber and she shows me her marks. I never noticed them before, because they're down near the floor, where she sleeps in the winter. She makes the marks with a charred stick, and every year at the midwinter full moon she washes the wall and starts over.

Grandmother's way of counting will let anyone see my paintings in the right order. I can make marks like hers on the backs of my clay slabs, in red paint. She saw the answer so fast! I hope I will be that wise when I'm older. Mother often tells me how important the elders are, but the ideas you remember longest are the ones that help you directly.

My first painting will be of the man with his bright light, painted in yellow, which works for sunlight. I'll try it on a broken piece first. The light made it hard to see his face, so I remember the way he looks better from the first time I dreamed of him, when Mother and I were together. His smile was nice, and his eyes looked friendly. He looked surprised to see me, but I probably looked surprised myself.

22

A FRIGID MORNING. I know this is the far north, but *so* cold, in June? I am out of the sack by five, underslept and desperate for coffee. I'm usually first up, but today I find Joel huddled around our tiny stove using our scarce butane to warm his hands. My irritation softens when he turns his face to me, because his problems are obviously bigger than mine.

"I slept about an hour," he says, by way of good morning—this is his normal level of social adeptness. "I had one of the scariest dreams of my life."

Already it begins. And I thought he might not notice the ceremonial chamber. I simply start making coffee. I know he will continue.

"I dreamed I went into the ceremonial chamber. I couldn't keep my balance and sat down to avoid falling.

The stream rose and could have carried me away, but it chose to subside instead. I passed out—I dreamed of passing out—and knew I was dying, but I woke up. Really woke up. About two. Since then I've been sorry I came here. I even thought about packing up and leaving, but that's absurd. I'm a grown man, and I don't believe in fairy tales."

I mean-spiritedly rejoice in his suffering. When the coffee is ready, I pour a cup for each of us and sit across from him. "Joel, the previous owners visited the cave once, in 1955. It bothered their dreams for the rest of their lives. It affects me and Roger and Mira all differently, but yours is the first real nightmare."

"What do you dream of?"

"The original people. The ceremonial chamber. Mira saw a woman painting the wall of the living chamber. All of us have lost sleep."

"I can't function without sleep. I had planned to stay a few days to watch the three of you work, but now I think I'll leave tonight, before dark. I'll sleep in the car and drive tomorrow morning."

Roger and Mira are here now, listening. "That's the thing about this cave," Mira says. "The ceremonial chamber does things to you. Leaving won't help. I had dreams in Baltimore. You want to know what I think?"

Joel doesn't care what Mira thinks, but he listens.

"I think you had a bad dream because you threatened to stop this project. I think that damn chamber is aware, at some level."

Joel looks at Mira to see whether she's serious. Then he shrugs his shoulders and pours more coffee. I try hard to suppress my feelings of sympathy. He *did* threaten to stop the project.

I HATE HAVING JOEL AROUND watching us work. I'd like to help him to his car as soon as breakfast is over. Roger and Mira think he'll do what's right because he'll fear nightmares otherwise. So he stays, and he drives me nuts. He tries to keep out of the way, but he's making mental notes for the story and wants to see everything we're doing. In his shoes I would do the same, but I can't work with him around, and I don't trust him out of my sight. Roger and Mira simply ignore him.

Joel glances frequently at the passage to the ceremonial chamber, obviously wanting to return there. I herd him in the other direction, staying near Mira to photograph her work, as if that were necessary. Mira knows it's not and repeatedly nudges me out of the way.

Every minute that I worry about Joel is wasted time, and we have a great deal to do. I force myself to focus and start collecting my gear. Roger understands why I've been stalling and is relieved that I'm ready to return to the survey. I'm surprised Joel doesn't ask to go with us.

Working with Roger restores my balance, and when we return to the living chamber hours later, Joel is gone. "He'll be back in a few weeks," Mira says. "He told me more about his dream. It really upset him, but he's fascinated that the ceremonial chamber has such power. We've had weeks to get used to the idea. Joel's in shock."

AFTER DINNER I stretch out on my bag to take stock of myself.

My usual way of reacting to psychological stress is to rev up, get overtired, sleep poorly, and end up sick. And sometimes start drinking. That won't happen on this trip, because our two six-packs are long gone. My problem now is sleeplessness.

All day today I have felt like a junkie shaking for lack of a fix. In what little sleep I had last night, my dreams were fragmented and troubling. I slept well in the ceremonial chamber two nights ago and would have gone back last night if Joel hadn't been here.

The stream beside our camp comes directly from the ceremonial chamber, and its sound reminds me of my contact with a young girl from long ago. I feel the chamber's presence even here and realize that I am finally near sleep.

> I am astonished to see the entire entry cavern open to the shelf, as it must have been before the collapse, its high ceiling shading a streamside

wildflower garden. In the rear, in an open area near the cave entrance, an older woman sits on a bench painting a pot. She is olive-skinned, with dark hair going grey in a curly froth. Her face is so like Alice's that she can only be her grandmother, although Alice's skin is lighter.

A second older woman appears, tiny and slim, with white hair. The two laugh together—and I can hear them!

I realize I am dreaming, that the dream is a gift from these two wise women. Their voices sound familiar, and all at once I know their history and their role. They are the alpha females—I see it in their faces, postures, behavior. They have lived here together since they were young. They have children here, and grandchildren.

No one else is in sight, but young voices shriek and laugh somewhere in the distance. A man joins the women; he is younger, tall, light-skinned, tow-headed. His deference to them is obvious even from a distance.

I wake with a start, still lying on my bag in camp, chilled. Roger and Mira have gone to bed. I wanted to sleep in the ceremonial chamber tonight, but I am exhausted. I think briefly of the dream. I could hear the women's voices!

Groggy with sleep, I take off my shoes and crawl into my bag.

A child comes from the cave. Alice! She is excited and happy, and carries a pottery tablet to show her grandmother.

Alice starts back toward the cave entrance. On an impulse, I follow, walking into the open cavern. No breakdown stands in my way. When Alice disappears into the cave, I duck through the entrance behind her.

Wait! There is so much light! With the entry in full daylight, the entire living chamber is dimly lit. I see only two hearths, but a third is well begun. Some of the walls haven't yet been painted!

This is the cave as Alice knew it.

Alice walks the length of the living chamber. I follow her up the passage to the ceremonial chamber and then down to the pool. She goes to the upstream flowstone where she and I first met—her private spot. I stop short of her, near the hearth—unchanged in five thousand years.

I wonder—how did I get down here in the dark? I realize I'm dreaming, but I'm more than a dream observer; I am actually in the ancient time.

Alice turns toward me, and in my forty-two years I have not before been so shaken by a look. Her young face is unguarded but as deep as a clear pool, childlike and yet wise. We share a smile, and the delight in her face reflects my own.

She looks at me occasionally as she marks her tablet with a charred stick. She is sketching me!

Another gift, this dream, and from Alice. What can I possibly give her in return? My pockets are empty, but on my belt is an aluminum carabiner-style key ring. As Alice watches, I unclip it and lay it beside me.

I feel my body relax. I realize I have been rigid and tense since I first saw this cave. A sensation of peace overwhelms me. I look again toward Alice; she is curled up asleep.

I WAKE in the ceremonial chamber. I can feel the corner of the hearth and hear the room's echoes exactly as in the dream, and no other place has such presence. The dream felt so real that I'm not surprised, but how did I get here? And how will I get out, without light? The route up the breakdown is familiar and short, so I should be able to find the tunnel, but then I'll have to negotiate the entire living chamber in the dark. Mira will kill me. Seriously.

When I emerge from the tunnel into the living chamber, my dismay abates, and I make my way slowly and carefully toward the dimly-visible entrance, thankful that morning light through our new entryway has saved me from Mira's wrath.

When I arrive at the tents, Roger looks at me with a puzzled smile. "When I got up, I realized you weren't in your bag and didn't have your helmet. I went looking and found you in the ceremonial chamber. I have no idea how you got there, but you were sleeping like a baby at the hearth. I decided not to wake you. I left you one of my flashlights. I guess you didn't see it. We can pick it up next trip."

It's eight in the morning, and I feel relaxed and well slept. But how on earth did I get over the breakdown to the entrance? And how did I get through the living chamber and into the ceremonial chamber? I wasn't even wearing shoes.

And my key ring is missing.

ONCE AGAIN I SAW HIM in the spirit chamber. I know his name now: Jered. And he left me a gift.

For the first time, he wore no hood. His hair is dark, but cut short. His beard was short, as if he had cut it off recently, and it had just started to regrow. He had a nice smile, but his face looked like a boy's.

Why would a man cut his beard and cut his hair short? I can't tell how old he is, but not young. Perhaps twenty-five.

We smiled at each other as we stood there, both of us enjoying the meeting. I felt I could touch him if I were close enough. I know Jered was there at another time, but everything that happens in the spirit chamber lasts forever. Grandmother and Aunt Inge believe they were the first people ever in this cave, so I think Jered will come to the spirit chamber later. But time makes no difference to the spirit.

I know Jered's gift wasn't accidental, because he looked at me as he put it down on the rock, beside the hearth. I found it when I woke, and it wasn't there before I slept. That seems impossible, but Mother has always told me the spirit is a mystery to everyone.

I am holding the gift in my hand. It is as real as the rocks, but I don't know what it is or even what it's made of. It is shaped like a ring, too big to fit a finger but smaller than my bracelet. Hard, like redmetal, but a different color. It shines softly in daylight, but I suppose it might grow dull and green in time, as redmetal does.

I feel magic in it. Something for me, from Jered.

WHEN I LEAVE THE CAVE I find Grandfather at the redmetal work area. He is alone. I hand him Jered's gift without a word.

"Alys, it's like a ring. Where did you get it?"

"In the spirit chamber. I dreamed of the man again. He made sure I was watching and then left this for me. I found it when I woke."

Grandfather turns it in his hand and holds it in bright sunlight. "It wasn't cast or worked with hammers, but it's perfectly smooth, except here, and here—"

As he presses on the ring, a gap appears—one part of the ring swings aside. "It opens!" Grandfather is obviously surprised. "It has a hinge." As he hands the ring to me, it closes again. I can barely press it open. It tries so hard to close that it threatens to pinch my finger.

Aunt Inge and Uncle Sigurd are here now, both curious. I hand the ring to Uncle Sigurd, who holds it very close to his eyes—he often complains about his vision. As Grandfather shows him how the ring opens, I tell Aunt Inge about the dream.

"The ring is from his time," she says. "Of course it is a circle. The spirit is enclosing you and him—and all of us—for some purpose."

"That is exactly what worries me." I did not hear Mother walking up to us. "I too know the spirit. Its power has always worked to our advantage, but I fear how it could affect Alys's life."

"Ana, the circle shows that Alys was right, that she and this man have something to do together."

"His name is Jered."

Mother looks pained. "How did you learn *that*?"

"Mother, I told you—I will be safe if I follow the spirit. Jered knows my name, too."

"Alys," Aunt Inge says, "do you actually speak with him?"

"Not yet, but I think we could."

"Look at this!" Uncle Sigurd has been examining the ring. "It has three parts, of two different materials—one for the body of the ring and the leg, but another for the hinge. The body and leg are attached to the hinge by tiny pins. Look!" He is very excited.

Grandfather looks closely. "I would like to know how those pins are made and attached."

"Zoan!" Grandmother Quitana is here now. She laughs. "A miracle occurs, and you hardly notice!"

"Hardly notice? *Look* at the workmanship! Amazing!"

"A gift to our granddaughter from another time! That's the miracle. Not how it happens to be made."

Grandmother is teaching Grandfather the same way she teaches me. The ring captures his imagination, but he does not see the meaning behind it, and she is determined to make him understand.

WHILE THE ELDERS TALK, others crowd around, drawn by the excitement. They pass the ring from hand to hand. "Please," I say anxiously, "be careful."

I speak too late. I am horrified to see the ring fall to the ground. It bounces away, and before I can react, my five-year-old brother Alwyn scoops it up and runs, chased by other youngsters. Panic seizes me, but Aunt Inge's hand is gentle on my shoulder. She starts toward the shrieking children, now fighting over who gets to hold the treasure. She quickly separates them and retrieves the ring, and I can breathe again.

Aunt Inge knows better than any of the others how much Jered's gift means to me. She smiles and presses it into my hand, and when she hugs me I burst into tears.

A quiet muttering begins among the adults. They all know I regularly spend time in the spirit chamber, but some haven't heard of Jered or the ring. What will they think when they hear that it was made in a different time? I don't care, as long as the people most important in my life understand. Mother is anxious for my safety, but she will come to see this event as a turning point in my life. Perhaps in all our lives.

The ring feels warm as I hold it. I will wear it around my neck on a length of braided hide. I feel Jered in it.

MANY OF MY CLAY SLABS break in the oven, but I now have three that are baked and ready to paint. Some of the slabs that broke had my sketches on them, outlines made with a knife blade. Grandmother Quitana thinks scratching into the damp clay weakens it, so I won't do that again.

I'm nervous about painting pictures of Jered. I want them to be perfect, but he has been different each time—once wearing a hood and once with a bright light hiding his face. I didn't see him clearly until today. I will save one slab for him and paint it soon, with a picture of his face on each side. One side will have the blinding light. That slab will be the only one without a number.

My other pictures will be easier. One is sketched already, of Mother and Grandmother Quitana and Aunt Inge, all my teachers. Another will be of Father and Grandmother Folke.

I will need many more slabs. Grandmother and I made four today, and Grandfather will bake them next time the oven is hot. I want a picture of our six elders together, to show my own grandchildren. I want one of Aunt Inge and Uncle Sigurd with their children and grandchildren, and one of Grandmother and Grandfather with theirs, not including me, because I will be painting it. Also Uncle Geyr and pregnant Aunt Angela, and the ceremony where Uncle Aramel and Aunt Eydis were married. And one of all the little children together.

Later I will want other pictures.

Paintings on the cave wall are never disturbed, but I will have to find a safe place for the finished slabs. I will display some of them, but I want people who come later to see them all, so they can know who we are and how we live.

I want Jered to find them. Now when I make a painting, it's for him.

ROGER AND I are dirty and tired after a day of surveying when we clamber out of the tunnel to find Mira sitting on the cave floor with her head in her hands.

Roger goes to her. "You OK?"

Her drawn face gives us the answer. "I can't do this. My list of work grows every day. I'm so tired I'm not sure what I'm seeing anymore. I can't believe we thought we might finish this season."

"Mira," I say, "we've talked about this. We all know we'll need another trip to finish."

"Jarrett! You don't understand. There is only one of me. Documenting what I can see now would take two or three years, and every day I uncover more. This is a project for a class of ten, not a lone ranger. These people lived here for generations, and they left tons of stuff.

Even a team working every day couldn't finish in the time we have."

"So we'll do less than full documentation. We don't have two or three years." I know this is not news to her. We must all earn a living.

Mira's temper flares. "Well then, let's pack it in right now and go home!" Her face is red. She couldn't mean it, not the thorough professional she is.

"Let's call it a day, have dinner, and get a good night's sleep. Everything will look better in the morning."

"Don't patronize me. Nothing will change overnight. The job still won't be possible tomorrow."

Roger has been quiet, and I'm grateful when he weighs in. She sags against him when he puts his arm around her shoulders, and the tears begin. Mira does not normally respond to stress by crying.

"There's more here than fatigue and time limits. Right?" Roger looks up at me and I get the message to leave them alone. That suits me; I have my own emotional problems and can't deal with hers. I think she will come around. She has a lot at stake. I can go anywhere and take pictures of caves, but for her this one is a once-per-lifetime gift.

REPLAYING THIS SCENE in my mind later, as I admire the view eastward from the cliff edge, I realize that Mira's outburst upset me. Her talk of leaving triggered something, almost panic. I am not ready to be cut off from this place when my contact with Alice has only begun.

Contact with Alice! I have accepted the dream events without pausing for reflection, but now their meaning hits me full force. If I'm not losing it completely, I must accept that I have misunderstood the rules that govern the universe. Leaving in the face of such an epiphany is unthinkable.

If Mira were in my place, she would realize we could learn more about these people from Alice than we ever could from paintings and artifacts.

Perhaps weeks of stress have driven me around the bend. Time will tell.

BY THE TIME ROGER AND MIRA EMERGE, it's almost dark, and I've been lost in thought for hours. All of us are exhausted and hungry and unhappy. We cook dinner in silence. I glance at Mira, but Roger catches my eye and shakes his head.

I know. Wait until she's ready to talk. Sometimes a man is glad to be single.

Steaks and brew would go well tonight, but what we have is freeze dry as usual—and no beer, which is good. I might put away too much and be sorry later.

I'm so distracted that I almost miss Mira's quiet sigh.

"I knew from the beginning that I couldn't finish in the time we have." She says this to the floor, without looking at me or Roger. "What I didn't know was what this place would do to me."

Long silence. I bite my tongue, and eventually she goes on.

"I've been studying a series of paintings of a big event—the arrival of three new people, and the battle on the cliff. We've talked about your photo of that scene, Jarrett, but the paintings convey the feeling of the moment better. They're large and incredibly detailed. Two people worked on them, and the paintings they did together all have more detail than the ones they did alone."

At last she looks up at me, but I see she is here in body only. Her mind is a million miles away. Or maybe five thousand years away.

"This morning I stood where the painters stood— the same people who fought the battle—and I fell in. One minute I was looking at the paintings, and the next I was there. I saw the scene unfold. The newcomers were exhausted and helpless on a ledge halfway down to the river. Two young couples lived here at that point, the founders. I recognized all four from the earlier paintings. Three of them were down on the ledge; a pregnant woman stayed up on the cliff. The three fought off a much larger group of armed warriors, who ran at them from below. I know it sounds crazy, but I was there. I heard the yelling and screaming. The violence stunned me."

She finishes with a telling afterthought. "The sun was in my eyes. It had just risen. The paintings don't show that."

MY TURN TO BE SILENT. A few months ago this story would have scared hell out of me, but after meeting Alice, I am ready to believe anything. Mira is shaken.

"Jarrett, I can't work this way. I have to be detached to produce valid results. Interpreting all this evidence is hard enough for a dispassionate observer. If I'm personally involved it will be impossible."

She pauses. "I feel like I'm getting crazy. I'm frightened."

I hesitate, unsure where to begin. "I don't know whether your experience was a delusion coming from loss of sleep, or a waking dream of the sort we've all experienced, or whether it's like my contact with Alice, a spirit phenomenon. In any case, it obviously comes from the work you're doing. Maybe that's because you spend all your time in the living chamber, where generations of people lived—people who believed they left their imprint on the places they loved. The emotions in there must be off-scale—births, deaths, and everything in between."

Mira is interested, and her body relaxes when she realizes I don't think she's crazy, so I go on. "I think it would help you to spend time in the ceremonial chamber." This is my main point, and the rest is easy. "The quiet and calm are like nothing I've known. The place restores body and spirit. They probably brought their sick and injured there to heal."

"I'm ready to try anything. I'll take the day off tomorrow and spend it there."

"You'd sleep better tonight if you went there now." I don't say it, but I suspect much of her stress is from sleeplessness.

Mira nods, and our crisis has passed. She and Roger spend the night in the ceremonial chamber while I bed down in camp. I actually do sleep, and dream as usual of the people who lived here long ago.

THE SUN IS HIGH when I wake. My companions are nowhere to be seen. I eat and suit up. As I enter the cave, they emerge from the ceremonial chamber.

Mira is a different person. "I saw the painters at work," she says, in great excitement. "Our two women. I knew them already, from the battle scene and many other paintings of them at different ages. Look over here." We walk to an early picture, and she points to a painting of two women. "They're young. The blonde one in particular. Let me show you a later picture." We walk to the back wall. "Another artist painted these. Here they are, older, the same women."

I hadn't looked closely at these paintings before. The figures are unmistakable. These are my alpha females. "I know them," I tell Mira, "I told you about them. I think they were the founders. The tall one is Alice's grandmother."

She points to the smaller woman. "This one fought alongside the two men in the battle I saw. Alice's grandmother was on the cliff, pregnant. Both of them appeared in my dream last night. When I woke, I wrote the main points of the dream." She takes out her phone, finds the entry, and hands it to me to read.

July 18 3:30 a.m.

I am in the spirit chamber, dreaming of them because they too knew the spirit. They bore their children in this room, and their grandchildren were born here. My vision of them fighting was a gift. I saw it because I immersed myself in the paintings. The spirit is powerful but benign. I must trust myself and show others the paintings.

Spirit chamber! What a great name.

MIRA IS RESTORED. She slept twelve hours and is full of energy, almost manic. "I'm doing the wrong thing. If I can't finish on this trip, why am I going through the living chamber in such detail? I should assemble data for a preliminary paper, a description of the cave and the people, plus a design for a full-on study project. The first paper will have photographs and descriptions of the major features—the living chamber, the hearths, the smelting oven, and the paintings. I could finish that much this summer."

"Don't leave out the spirit chamber." I don't add that I suggested such a paper yesterday.

We are standing at the back of the living chamber. Roger has been wandering, and is minutely inspecting a painting on the back wall, near the northwest corner. "Jarrett, look at this!"

He has found a map of the cave. We didn't recognize it before, because it isn't drawn as modern cave maps are. It is clear, however, and has fine lines and great detail. It shows that we know only a small portion of the cave. Roger is excited. "Look. The rock stacks in the maze are marked with crosses. And here's another entrance, at the west end. That slit passage! It was open once!"

We had guessed. We found a large room, dimly lit from above, with fire scars but no artifacts. A slit going further west was blocked with breakdown. It must have led to an entrance once. Why else would there have been fires in a room so far into the cave?

Over a late breakfast we talk about the state of our project. Half our time here is spent—we still plan to wrap up in early September. We've made good progress, and it helps us to concede that we can't finish this summer. Mira has a mountain of data and is eager to start toward her preliminary paper. Roger and I will finish surveying the lower levels and do as many upper passages as we can, although today we'll examine the place where there was once another entrance.

As I gather my gear to return to surveying, I hear Roger and Mira laughing together. We're no longer in crisis, but we're still playing with emotional dynamite. And I have a feeling that some drama lies ahead.

GRANDFATHER IS GONE from us forever, and I cannot bear it.

Every moment of this day pains me, for I cannot escape the truth. My life is forever changed, and without warning. I feel I will never be a child again. Of course I come to the spirit chamber for comfort, but the wound is still too raw for any healing, and I simply lie sobbing in the dark, unable to think of life without him.

The sound of the stream calms me, but I feel like a bird who has lost a wing. I have depended on him more than I realized—on his skills and knowledge and overflowing love. Perhaps he loved all his children and grandchildren equally, but he always made me feel like his special favorite. And now he is gone.

I finger the ring as it hangs around my neck on its cord of hide. Thinking of Grandfather and his curiosity about how it was made brings Jered to mind. I wish he could know what has happened. He could never understand my loss, but I sense a strength in him that would help me at this awful time.

Grandfather was so excited about the ring! He was so alive!

MOTHER AND GRANDMOTHER QUITANA woke me this morning, and their stricken faces terrified me. They said nothing—they were beyond speaking—but simply led me to where Grandfather lay cold on his sleeping pallet. He was not sick. He had no injury. I ran screaming from him, but Aunt Inge led me back to cry over him. Aunt Angela was there, but Uncle Geyr is away hunting, with Father and others. Uncle Sigurd was there, in tears. We all sat together in silent sorrow, and the little children gathered around us, frightened and unsure.

Star lay at Grandfather's side. She knew too. That was a terrible time.

Aunt Inge finally stood.

"Tonight the hunters will return, and tomorrow we will carry Zoan to the spirit chamber and pray over him. Then we will carry him outside and bury him on the Benchland he loved. He found this place, he and Quitana. They were the first of us to stand here, and it is here we will say our last goodbye to him."

Spirit Chamber

I EMERGE FROM THE SPIRIT CHAMBER, wrung out of tears and shaking with exhaustion, to find that Father has returned. Mother sits with him quietly while he absorbs our loss. Grandmother Quitana sits beside our fire, looking tired and alone, and I forget my own grief and go to her.

"Alys," she says, "you must try to feel him around us. He is here still. His spirit will be here forever, and the spirit chamber will help you find him." Her eyes are red from crying all day.

"We were not so much older than you are when we came here." She stands and turns to the open cavern mouth. "He and I stood right here in the snow—it was freezing, and we were too cold to stay outside long— and I recognized the place from a dream. We were eighteen, and I was pregnant with Angela."

She and Grandfather knew each other as children. And I have been feeling sorry for myself? Aunt Inge pulls Grandmother into a long silent embrace. Grandfather's death is terrible for us all. Still, I feel singled out for pain. I have never known such a loss. Mother has lost two babies, and we all suffered, as we always do when babies die, but not like this. My unhappiness feels like forever.

I RETURN TO THE SPIRIT CHAMBER to play my flute, the flute Father brought for me from Rivermouth along with the puppies. It is made of the bone from a bird's leg. It has seven holes, and it plays a note when you blow into it, depending on which holes are covered. The sound is softer than singing and the notes are pure. I love the flute and play it every day, and today its music comforts me.

I see torchlight and look up to discover Mother and Aunt Inge climbing down toward me. They sit near me and listen while I try to play one of Mother's prayer songs. Aunt Inge takes my arm. "Will you play tomorrow, while we sing prayers for your grandfather?"

I'm not sure I can play while I'm crying, but I'll try.

I want Jered to know. Perhaps the ring he gave me will help me find him.

I DREAM OF DESPAIR—Alice's, not my own.

> *Alice is in the spirit chamber, lying on her rock, sobbing. I haven't seen her since I left my key ring for her, and at the time she seemed a happy youngster. Could I be the cause of her distress? I feel that she is thinking of me—but not only me. Something terrible has happened to her.*

I wake acutely anxious—not in the spirit chamber, but in my bag in camp. My watch says midnight, and the night is dark, with blazing stars. Should I go to the spirit chamber? Was Alice calling me? I can't stay awake long enough to decide.

I WAKE ABRUPTLY, alert to the sound that woke me—the scuffing of footsteps from the direction of the cave. Someone—something—is coming, and in an instant I am afraid.

The last quarter moon has risen since I woke at midnight, and in its light I see a figure coming toward the tents from the cave.

Alice?

Questioning my sanity, I look around to clear my head. Our camp seems normal. The sounds of gentle snoring come from Roger and Mira's tent. But the approaching child is of another world. I am wide awake now, heart pounding.

She stands in the moonlight, looking toward the camp. She too seems afraid, for she clutches impulsively at something around her neck. A talisman?

What can she possibly think of our tents? No wonder she's afraid.

Alice comes up to me and extends a hand, and I see that what she had been holding is my key ring. Her eyes are swollen and red from crying, and I think of my dream of her sobbing in the spirit chamber.

None of this is possible, but for lack of any other option, I simply surrender to what is happening and wait to see where it leads.

ALICE TAKES MY HAND and tugs me insistently toward the cave. I slip on shoes and follow her through the open cavern—not closed off by breakdown—and into the living chamber as I saw it once before, with only two—no, now three complete hearths, casting long shadows in the moonlight that passes through the cave entrance.

How is it that I am in the ancient time? Alarms ring in my mind.

Alice leads me into the spirit chamber. I emerge from the tunnel into a scene I never expected to see: a ceremony is in progress. Dozens of people are seated around the pool, children and adults. Lighted torches surround the group, and a small fire burns in the hearth. I scan the crowd, but I cannot find Alice.

I understand why I'm here when I see the body. An older man lies beside the pool in a ring of flowers. His dark hair is greying. He is dressed in leather.

Alice has brought me to a funeral service. The entire colony is here. I sit where I entered, at the top of the breakdown, wishing desperately for a camera.

I spot Alice, in her private place on the upstream flowstone, with her mother, her grandmother, and the tiny white-haired woman. Alice stands and begins to play a small bone flute. She fingers it to produce a melody. Whispers around the room die down, and the room falls silent but for the sound of the stream and the haunting tune from the flute.

Alice's mother stands and sings along with the flute. At one point she raises both arms. As one, every person in the group echoes the gesture, and I realize the song is a ritual prayer. The group forms a line, and each person comes to the side of the dead man, looks at him, and bows or kneels. Some touch him. Alice's grandmother holds both his hands. Is he her husband,

Alice's grandfather? Several people break out crying, but the song continues, with voice and flute.

This image will never leave me—the silent mourners, the body, the spirit chamber, the torches, the fire, Alice's tear-stained face. Despite the beauty of the place and the music, it is the saddest occasion imaginable.

"JARRETT?"

Mira gently shakes me awake. "Are you OK? You were crying. Really sobbing." She and Roger have a fire going. It is not yet five in the morning, but dawn is well underway.

My face is wet with tears, and my head swims with images, not at all dreamlike, but scenes from concrete recent memory. How can I ever explain it? I have spent the night in another world. I tell what I saw as we eat breakfast. The sadness remains poignant and terrible— I too suffered that loss—but the unearthly beauty of the setting and the ceremony will remain with me for life.

A HALFMONTH NOW since Grandfather died, and I have been feeling guilty for spending so much time thinking about Jered. Today Aunt Inge comes to me in the spirit chamber to talk about it. As usual, she knows my mind. Even more than Mother.

"Alys, rejoice that you met him." Aunt Inge always comes directly to the point. "You and he have a task to do together. He looks friendly, and the spirit would not allow harm."

Aunt Inge is the only one who knows Jered was here for Grandfather's funeral ceremony. She saw me watching him, and that gave him away. Even Mother didn't notice. He was really here, and I was awake, not dreaming. His gift to me brought him here. I took his hand and led him into the spirit chamber.

When I have my own pouch I will keep the ring in it. Until then I'll wear it around my neck. I always sense him in it.

"I want to show Jered my painting of him with the bright light. I'll sleep here tonight. Mother knows and doesn't object."

"I talked to her about it. She sent venison. Yrsa always said food is important in the spirit chamber." Aunt Inge gives me a hide bag and then hugs me before leaving.

Aunt Inge often speaks of Yrsa, her teacher, Uncle Geyr's grandmother. Thinking of her makes Aunt Inge cry. Yrsa was a powerful woman, a healer. When Grandfather and other men were badly hurt by a bear, Yrsa healed them all, including her husband, Bjorn. Our Bjorn is named for him. Yrsa discovered the pool for cleaning redmetal. She was the midwife for Aunt Angela's birth, and Uncle Geyr's. Mother's, too, although Mother doesn't remember her.

Aunt Inge says Yrsa and I could have taught each other in the spirit chamber. I feel Yrsa every time I come here.

I ALWAYS BRING THE FLUTE here. I play Mother's spirit chamber prayer for a long time before I lie back and yield to the sound of the stream.

Jered sits by the hearth, listening to me play the prayer song. When I stop, he smiles and puts an imaginary flute to his lips. I play the song again.

As I play, the spirit shows me what I must do. I pick up the clay slab with the painting of Jered. Only one side is done so far, showing him with the light.

He follows me away from the stream. We crawl into the neighboring chamber, which is also beautiful but has no stream. People come here to use the pool that cleans redmetal, but I think only Mother and I have seen the whole chamber. Jered follows me to the rear corner of the room and onto a high shelf. Against the wall is a perfect place for my clay slabs, a recess in the rock where I've hidden things from the other children for years. No one knows about it but me. And now Jered.

He watches me put the clay slab into my hiding place.

I wake in my spot. The clay slab lies beside me, but when I'm through painting both sides I'll leave it there for him.

WE HAVE BEEN HERE only two months, but the emotional turmoil makes the time seem longer. Mira has retreated from the brink of nervous collapse, but I'm more stressed out every day. The problem is dreams.

Before I came here I lived in the real world, where my dreams don't confuse themselves with daily life. Here, they are part and parcel of it, as real as breakfast. Alice seems like a young friend who happens to be with us on this expedition. Yes, I know she's from another world and another time. But that world is where I live when I sleep in the spirit chamber.

I need that world. I'm desperate for it. After a few nights away from the spirit chamber, I no longer sleep well. I am short-tempered with Mira and even Roger, who is hammered from two sides. I make elementary camera errors. I get paranoid. Three nights ago I woke up in a panic because our work wasn't properly backed up. Our only copies of the data—twenty thousand photographs and all our notes—were in camp. I got up in the middle of the night, wrote a fresh backup disk, climbed the rope, and tucked the disk into the truck. But what did I accomplish? Why is it any safer in the truck?

When this project ends in a few weeks, I will lose contact with Alice's world. What will become of me? Will my need for the spirit chamber conveniently end when I go home? My biggest fear is that it won't, and my anxiety grows as the remaining time dwindles.

OUR WORK GOES ON, as it must if we aren't to waste precious time. For the moment Mira seems content to collect data for her preliminary paper. She says she could do a respectable job with what she has now, and anything she gains from here forward is gravy.

Roger and I continue to survey the cave. The work is exhausting, not something we feel like doing day after day, but we both feel obligated to carry the survey as far as we can, even though the cave map in the living chamber shows that we have no hope of finishing this year. We discuss a second expedition, but all of us are painfully aware that it might not occur.

That map is remarkable. Some proportions are wrong, but not by much, and the cave is far more extensive than we knew. The main trunk is only a fraction. The upper levels alone are huge. In two months of hard work, we've mapped about three miles of lower-level passages. Looking at the map, I'd guess that's less than twenty percent of the cave. A full survey would take us many more summers. The ancient surveyor must have worked at it for years.

WILL I EVER ESCAPE the clutches of this project, or am I doomed to suffer lifelong craziness and insomnia? I worry about that. Except when I sleep in the spirit chamber, where I'm spending the night.

> *Alice is in her spot playing her flute. She faces the stream and does not look at me. The tune is hypnotic, and as she plays, I surrender to its spell. The stream sings with Alice, and her melody weaves patterns around the water's comforting incoherent chatter, ever changing but always the same.*

> *When she stops playing, I return slowly to Earth to find myself once again the object of her direct, unafraid gaze. She smiles when she sees I'm aware of her. I mime a flute to show her I would like to hear more. She returns to the melody, and she and spirit chamber disappear, leaving me in a world of spirit sound and music.*

> *The stream! The source of the spirit! It sings of where it has been and where it is going. Alice is teaching me!*

Time stops, but the music goes on. I learn that Alice will give me something that I lack, something I need before I can leave here. I know we have something to do together.

Alice stops playing and stands. She picks up a clay tablet and carefully protects it as she clambers over boulders. I follow her into an adjacent chamber, which Roger and I surveyed only a few days ago.

She leads me to the back wall, and we climb onto a shelf, where she holds out the clay tablet for me to see. A picture of me! With my light in her eyes. I still regret that time.

She puts the tablet into a recess in the shelf, a long shallow crevice against the cave wall.

I wake exhilarated. Alice has left something for me!

I SLEEP DEEPLY in the spirit chamber, feeling sheltered, but waking is harsh, like the trauma of a newborn, precipitated from the protective warmth of the womb into the cold world. This time the shock of waking is overwhelmed by the urgent need to find the place Alice showed me. I pick up my mag lite—I haven't used the helmet light in here since I shined it into her eyes. I follow the red tape road into the adjoining chamber and then to the back wall, where Mira's pathway doesn't reach. The place is exactly as it was in the dream.

Exactly as in Alice's time. The constancy of caves is a comfort.

I climb onto the shelf. Roger and I aimed our lights back into here but saw no leads and pressed on. I work my way to where the shelf meets the wall and shine the light into the recess where Alice put the tablet.

What I see makes me dizzy. I am shocked. Dozens of clay tablets. Maybe a hundred. Sitting here for five thousand years, in two separate natural cubbyholes.

I PICK UP the closest tablet. It is about the size of a magazine—not fragile, but sturdy. The edges and corners are rough rather than precise. The image is an exquisite portrait of a woman—her face only. I know the artist, but who was the subject? She resembles Alice, with dark curly hair and dark eyes. Her sister? Her mother? Yes! I remember her mother from my first dream of Alice, in the spirit chamber. I saw the mother again at the funeral ceremony. Alice does strongly resemble her. But what I'm looking at is much too good to be the work of a little girl.

The back of the tablet has eight circles and three straight strokes, painted in red:

O O O O O O O O I I I

The next tablet is a painting of the same woman, but with a man, blond, tall. Alice's father? On the back is another set of marks: again eight circles, but only two straight strokes.

A numbering system! Alice! You amaze me!

And me without a camera. I must fix that immediately. I carefully replace the two tablets and hustle toward the exit and camp.

"MORE PAINTINGS!"

I arrive in the middle of Roger and Mira's breakfast. They are up early. Both look ragged, but Mira comes alive in an instant. "Where?"

"In the big room south of the spirit chamber. Roger and I surveyed it last week. Alice showed me in a dream where to look. She put paintings there, on clay tablets. Lots of them. Maybe a hundred. I looked at two, both portraits of people's faces. Artistically they're better than the paintings on the walls in the living chamber. Beautiful. I'm on my way back with a camera."

Naturally, they both want to come with me.

Today is the turning point in our project. I can feel it. The finding of the tablets is what I've been waiting for.

As I eat my freeze-dried fruit, I remember learning in the dream that Alice would give me something I needed to finish up. With the pictures of the tablets, I'll be ready to go home and publish.

AFTER BREAKFAST we drag my cameras and one of the big stand lights into place. The batteries are fresh—our portable solar chargers have worked fine—and I will have almost an hour of light, far more than I'll need. I'll turn the lights on for each shot and off in between.

We start with the two tablets I've already seen. Under the LED light the paint looks as fresh as if it had been applied last week. I shoot both sides of each one.

I show Roger and Mira the numbers. "Incredible," Mira says. "Can I take this out, now, please? Just this one?"

Roger leaves with her. Mira has taken off her sweatshirt and carries the tablet swaddled like a baby. It could not be in safer hands.

In a museum, I'm good for about an hour before everything begins to look the same, but I could look at Alice's paintings all day. Tablet after tablet shows that she was a talented and accomplished artist. The tablets make the wall paintings look—well, primitive. The two have similar colors, but the tablets have finer lines and delicate details of face and hair that are unlike anything in the living chamber.

The numbers get smaller as I go along. From eight circles it goes to seven circles and four straight strokes. Like Roman numerals! The circles represent five. The first group has 43 tablets, in order. The last is number one. The first tablet I pick up from the second group is number 44; I started in the middle.

I'm hungry—it's almost one in the afternoon—but I won't even consider stopping before I finish.

Roger brings lunch. I still have dozens of tablets to shoot, and I feel urgently that I must do them all now. Roger shakes his head at what I show him. "Mira thinks this is the greatest find of Neolithic art ever. She and I think the tablet she took—the beautiful woman—is Alice's mother. One of the wall paintings shows her with Alice as a toddler."

They have forgotten that I know Alice's mother from dreams. Yes. That's who it is.

I find a tablet that identifies Alice's mother as our cave mapper. Alice painted her standing beside the map, the pride in her stance coming through clearly.

I see a few people I recognize, including Alice's grandmother, in a picture of three older couples. And the small older woman I saw myself. I am flooded by images. Men building a house against a rock wall, near the river. A row of houses near the river. Deep snow on the shelf. A big black dog playing with two small children. Two older men, one blond, one dark-haired. I recognize them from the painting of the six elders. I see Alice's grandfather, whose funeral I attended. The founders! The alpha males!

I find many self-portraits—Alice at about the age I know her and then as a young woman. Later I see her with a man and a baby, and as a mother with three children I'm sure are hers.

The history of the colony, in pictures!

Near the end of the tablet stash, I find nearly a dozen tablets that are indecipherable, because the paint has crazed into a million fine lines. She must have used a different sort of paint. Tantalizing hints of images underlie the crazing, but I can't make anything of the details. I photograph the tablets anyway, hoping I'll be able to decipher them later.

The last tablet has two sides and no number. On one side is the picture I saw in the dream, of me with the helmet light. On the other is a picture of my face. I look like a man who's been camping out for two months.

As I try to absorb it all, I find the flute.

I EMERGE ABOUT SEVEN O'CLOCK—still late afternoon. I have the tablet with two pictures of me, the flute, and my cameras. I'll have to go back for the LED light panel. I'm ravenously hungry, but I feel like a new man, as if everything I've worried about is unimportant now. I've found what I was looking for.

My spirits are so high that I am not upset even when I discover that our camp has an extra person tonight. Joel Harte is back. Perhaps even with steaks and beer. Mira's tablet—the first one I found, showing Alice's mother—lies on my bag, and Joel is examining it.

"Jarrett, *look* at this. Stunning. Out of the class of the wall paintings." His excitement softens me toward him. "Mira says you found a hundred of these. That's the icing on the cake. I've been pushing the book. I sent descriptions to two publishers, and both are enthusiastic. Could you stand a big advance? It was already the hottest cave book since Lechuguilla, and now you find paintings like this one? The book will make a ton of money."

Without a word, I put the painting of my face beside the one of Alice's mother.

JOEL'S EYES WIDEN as he looks back and forth from my face to its 5,000-year-old likeness. I have never before seen him actually speechless.

Before he recovers, I turn my tablet over so the helmet-light image is up. I put the flute beside it. "You can't have this tablet or the flute, Mira. They're mine. Personal gifts from the artist. This is the only tablet without a number. Yours is number 43 of 97. I have photos of all of them now."

Joel is still silent, perhaps thinking he's gotten off at the wrong exit, where everyone is insane. Roger and Mira are open-mouthed too, even though they already knew of my contact with Alice. We stand looking at the tablets and the flute for some time. Nobody says a word.

"Let's eat and do business," I say. "Long day, and I'm starved."

Joel's steaks taste incredible after two months of caver chow, and he did bring beer. After dinner, he turns back to Mira's tablet. "The girl painted this? Alice?" The question is rhetorical; he's still coming to terms with it. We had told him of Alice, but he didn't know the full story until now. "God!" he says. "We'll have to name the book Alice, I guess."

"Spirit Chamber," I say.

I have just opened my third can of beer when a big explosion rocks us.

NO, NO, NO!! What the hell happened?! I see the others shouting at me, but I can't hear them over the roaring in my head.

The echo of the boom and the sounds of falling rock die away slowly. My adrenaline takes longer to subside. Minutes later, when I see through the thinning dust cloud that the entrance is partly blocked, panic strikes me. I could be separated forever from the cave, the tablets, the spirit chamber. And Alice! I instinctively start for the entrance, but Roger stops me.

Joel is the first to put it together. "The quarry! It's the damn quarry! They're blasting!"

Why didn't I understand before? The breakdown in the entrance is new since 1955. The quarry probably does this every year.

"We have to stop it!" Joel is out of control, almost incoherent. He starts for the rappel rope.

Roger grabs his arm. "It's too dark for them to prepare another blast tonight. Sit down and cool off. We'll talk and decide what to do."

Joel barely hears him. "They might start again first thing tomorrow. They could wreck the cave! We have to *do* something." He seems completely invested in this project, and part of me is sorry I doubted him.

Roger is always the voice of reason. "They probably blast whenever they need to. We should find out whether they're finished."

"If I leave now, I can be there when they start tomorrow morning. I can stop them."

"Why would they stop because we ask them to? They wouldn't even let us climb from their property. They don't know the cave is here and wouldn't care if they did. The quarry is a business. The only way we'll stop them is by drawing the government into it."

We've been so careful not to advertise what we're doing! "Roger," I say, "that would end our project."

"We're done for this year anyway, and I no longer think we can keep the cave to ourselves. It's too important for that. We've been lucky to have the entire summer."

He's right, of course. "OK, Joel. Go. See what you can do. We can decide later about bringing in the government, depending on what you find. Meanwhile we'll wrap up and get ready to leave."

I LIE AWAKE long after Mira and Roger are asleep, thinking about everything that has happened. When I found the tablets I felt this project coming to a close.

Does it have loose ends I should tie up? What would I lose if a blast tomorrow morning closed the cave permanently? I packed the tablet and flute with great care, thinking about how I would feel if they were broken after five thousand years. I should go back to retrieve my LED light panel, forgotten in the flurry of events. Is it safe for me to return to the cave? There will be no blasting at night, but more rock could fall. The sooner I go, the better, and I mustn't stay long.

The panel sits near Alice's tablets. I look at a few and find a painting of Alice as a young woman, with a tall blond man and a baby. She looks happy. What would she think if she saw this? What better way to thank her and say goodbye than to show her this scene from her future?

The LED panel can wait. I wrap the tablet in my jacket, take off my helmet, grab the mag lite, and hustle to the spirit chamber, where I sit by the hearth and listen. I set the tablet beside me on the rock and lie back. As soon as I snap off the light I sense her presence. Once again, the sound of the stream leaves me totally relaxed.

> When I sit up, she sees the tablet on my lap. She steps toward me to look and sits beside me. I hand her the tablet, and she looks at it for a long time. She understands!

She turns back to me and looks into my eyes. There are tears on her face. She knows this is goodbye.

I wake seated, with the tablet in my hands. I put it down again, beside me, and lie back to reflect.

I WAKE WITH A START. Late morning! I had not intended to sleep though the night. I hurry to the adjoining chamber, return the tablet, pick up my helmet and LED panel, and move fast toward the exit.

As I approach the tunnel to the living chamber, Mira appears. She is in a panic.

"Joel found out a blast is coming! Right away, at nine! Run!" My watch says 8:58. The LED panel is awkward in the tunnel. "Leave the damn thing!" Mira's agitation is spiraling into the red. "Run!"

I drop the panel and run.

I hear the blast as I duck through the cave entrance. Mira is a few feet in front of me. I have never before seen her really sprint. A large boulder falls directly in front of her. She vaults over it and is out. I think I'm clear, but a rock the size of a volleyball hits me in the leg and knocks me down.

Hands grab mine; Joel and Roger drag me clear. Rocks are still falling. I stand and hobble into camp leaning on the two of them. As I sit, I feel a second blast—much bigger. Monstrous. I don't remember falling, but I am lying on my back on the ground.

I look in panic toward the cave and see the entire ceiling of the entry cavern collapse. Dust overwhelms everything and I can see no more.

MIRA HANDS OUT DUST MASKS. I gingerly test my leg; it will have a nasty bruise, but it seems to work. My caving suit took most of the damage from being dragged. Thank goodness I didn't have my cameras.

Over the next ten minutes, as gritty dust settles on every surface, including me, I strain unsuccessfully to see through the thinning cloud, dreading the inevitable confirmation of what I already know. I feel like a condemned man awaiting execution.

At last I can see. It's all over. The cave entrance is buried behind countless tons of rock.

I LIE BACK in the spirit chamber and close my eyes to wait. Listening to the stream, I understand that Jered will come here for the last time.

He sits at the hearth with something in his lap. I walk to him and lean over to look. One of my clay slabs! I sit beside him. He smiles and hands it to me. It shows a young woman, with a baby—and Kyle. That makes me look at the woman again. Me! Grown up, but still young. I'm sure I painted it myself.

Jered has found the clay slabs!

I stare at the painting for a long time. I've been sure about Kyle for months, ever since he was so sick, but this new knowing is from the spirit. Kyle and I will marry! This is our baby! I will paint this picture! I know where Jered found it, but it's not there yet. Jered will tell my story. But first he's showing me what lies ahead.

Before I hand the slab back, I try to memorize exactly how my baby will look. Healthy! Dark hair, dark eyes. Just a few months old. A girl, I think, but I'm not sure.

Jered stands and looks at me with a sad smile. We both know we will not see each other again.

When I wake, I am peaceful and happy. Jered and I have finished what we needed to do. I showed him where to find the slabs, and he found them. My most important problem is solved. Others will see my paintings and know our story.

And Kyle! My heart is joyful. Should I tell him? Should I tell Mother and Aunt Inge? I won't be fourteen for two more years.

How could I *not* tell them?

31

ONCE AGAIN, I get an unexpected call from Sweden.

This one comes from a functionary in the Swedish Ministry of Culture. He comes to the point quickly. "Mr. Eriksson, the Ministry has arranged a ceremony to mark the completion of its restoration work in Alice's Cave. Minister Engberg wishes to invite you to lead a group of guests and scientists through the cave on that occasion. The ceremony is scheduled for the twentieth of April. The Minister extends her greetings and her congratulations on your remarkable book. She hopes you can attend."

As he speaks, my eye falls on Alice's painting of me. The tablet is under glass on its pedestal in the middle of my living room, with the flute and Mira's statement that the paint is five thousand years old.

The Ministry has taken six years to reach this point and now gives me only six weeks notice? I agree, of course. Since the blast and rockslide I have seen the cave only in dreams and photographs, and I'm ready for another visit. Roger and Mira are too busy to go, and they spent weeks at the cave last summer, during the construction. Joel too is unavailable, which is fine with me.

My life has been peaceful since I left the cave. The book's success has let me reduce my work schedule. I sleep well now, although I still occasionally dream of Alice.

THE MINISTRY ACTED FAST when Mira and Joel appeared on their doorstep to ask them to stop the quarry from wrecking the cave. The government bought the quarry property, and the blast that closed the cave was the last. After that the Ministry did nothing for three years, although their archaeologists were surely aware of Mira's study results. What finally led to action was the publication of *Spirit Chamber*, with hundreds of photos of the cave and its artwork.

The current Minister was appointed about the time the book came out. She took a personal interest in the cave and appointed a committee to study the matter. A year later I sold my entire inheritance to the Swedish government for one dollar. Last summer the Ministry commissioned a project to dig out the entrance. I'd like to have seen the helicopter set heavy equipment down in our campsite, but I was on assignment in New

Zealand for a month. Mira was at the cave to keep the work away from potential archaeological sites out on the shelf. The Minister herself came there often, and she bombarded Mira with questions. Once the entry was open, Mira took her through the living chamber. I wept with relief when Mira told me nothing inside the cave was damaged, although the smelting oven in the entry cavern was reduced to rubble.

The day before the event, a very formal young man who speaks excellent English meets me at the Stockholm airport. He drops me at a hotel and will accompany me to the site tomorrow.

SEVEN OF US share the helicopter. Most of the others are journalists; this occasion will have first-class press coverage. The scientific team and the officials are already on site. We touch down where our tents stood.

"We will join the Minister's party inside the cave," our guide says. He hands out booties, gloves, and helmets—with lights, which relieves me; I had feared the government might have installed lighting.

The passage through the rockslide is big enough to admit a truck. The entry cavern, though, is filled with rubble nearly to the cave entrance, which appears unchanged except that it now has a massive steel gate.

The living chamber seems utterly familiar, as if I had never left. A dozen people are clustered near the wall, talking about the paintings, carefully staying within Mira's red tape pathways.

Our guide introduces me to the Minister.

"I'm pleased to meet you, Madam Minister." As I say it, though, I'm sure she and I already know each other.

Then I notice her helmet. Except for the two of us, the entire party has ill-fitting government helmets. Hers is obviously her own, a scarred veteran with a second light attached by duct tape. A caver!

She looks at me with a directness that unsettles me because it is all too familiar. "I'm honored to meet you, Mr. Eriksson. Please call me Alys."

Glossary of Names

Ancient characters and places

Ana, thirteen-year-old daughter of **Zoan** and **Quitana**, founders of the Benchland colony, who have three other living children: **Angela**, eighteen, **Druian**, sixteen, and **Aramel**, four.

Uncle Sigurd and **Aunt Inge**, colony founders, with four living children between four and thirteen: two boys, **Leif** and **Kyle**, and two girls, **Ragna** and **Eydis**.

Olaf, fifteen-year-old son of **Andor** and **Folke**.

Ingvar, Andor's brother.

Fedr, a widower responsible for his three small children, **Brandr**, **Dota**, and **Svala**, Fedr came early to the Benchland and soon married **Heidl**, widowed mother of the infant **Geyr**. Heidl died before this story opens.

Amena, Quitana's mother, who lives in **Northpoint**, where Zoan and Quitana grew up.

Meriel, Zoan's mother, who lives in Northpoint.

Karl, a boatmaker in the coastal village of **Rivermouth**.

Aodan, a childhood friend of Zoan, living in Northpoint.

Alys, daughter of Olaf and Ana.

Alwyn, son of Olaf and Ana.

Astrid, daughter of Druian and Ragna.

Bjorn, son of Geyr and Angela.

Acknowledgments

SHE HAS SUPPORTED US since we began writing four years ago. She took us seriously even though we assured her of our purely recreational intent, a myth we actually believed.

She finds time in her own hectic schedule to advise, teach, and encourage us. She reads what we write. She dived with enthusiasm into proofreading this book.

With an abundance of gratitude, we are happy to dedicate this volume to Joyce Gibson Roach.

WE WROTE the first version of *Spirit Chamber* in 2012 and distributed it to friends for comment. Many read it and encouraged us to press on. Our thanks to all. You know who you are.

THE PROOFREADING EVENT of July, 2015 was the best-attended yet, and yielded the richest harvest. Our readers are becoming editors, and we received as many wording suggestions as suspected errors—more than 300 comments from nearly two dozen readers. Ten readers will receive prize volumes for comments that resulted in substantive changes to the book: Willow Bunu, Chris Earnest, Eric Hosler, Mary Hosler, Louie Jaeckel, John David Lamb, Dan Lewis, Joyce Roach, Frances J. Sawaya, and Nicholas G. Williams.

We owe particular thanks to Frances J. Sawaya, who has generously given us the benefit of her professional skills for each of our four books.

WRITING is only part of what we do. We will soon have four books for sale, and they all demand promotion and publicity. We are a business, which means accounting, tax returns, and bank accounts. We have a web presence that requires maintenance and updating. We need working space. All of this places constant demand on Mary and Paul. They do what must be done, and Paul maintains our books and tax records besides. It goes without saying that without them we couldn't do what we do, and we are grateful indeed.

The Benchland Series

Book One

Rockslide

2014

Book Two

Spirit Chamber

Light from the Stream

Inheritance

2015

Book Three

Ring of Fire

Warriors

Child of Fire

2016

THE FIVE NOVEL-LENGTH STORIES of the Benchland series span more than fifty years of the history of the Benchland community, and the two stories of the third volume cover that entire time period. *Warriors*, the backstory of Sigurd and Inge, begins nine years before the discovery and founding of the Benchland. *Child of Fire* is a sequel to *Inheritance*. The following pages present excerpts of both stories.

All three volumes are now available in paperback and Kindle editions.

Warriors

1

HE WAS OUT COLLECTING FIREWOOD by dawn as usual. He wore his heavy cloak, for mornings were still cold even now that the snow was mostly gone, and the family would need a fire until midday.

Often he met other boys with their slings and baskets in the woods nearest the village, but it was nearly stripped of firewood now, and he was alone in the large forest farther upstream. He quickly picked up a full load from the wealth of storm-blown spruce branches. The green of the forest was vivid against heavy grey clouds, and the breeze had died away. Sigurd sensed an approaching storm, perhaps even a late snowstorm.

Afterward he realized that going to the farther forest had saved his life.

BEFORE STARTING FOR HOME, he sat on a fallen log beside the stream, at the edge of a large frost-covered meadow.

The village looked small in the distance, lying between two hills at the stream canyon's narrow mouth. Elvdal was its name—twelve houses west of the stream, which hugged the eastern hill as it left the canyon to flow out over the flats toward the river. The western hill hid his own house, which was far enough from the stream to be inconvenient, for Sigurd's chores included fetching water in hide bags. Smoke would be curling above the house; his mother had already started the fire when he left. His brother would be milking the goats, his little sister helping with breakfast.

Sigurd was the middle child, at thirteen a sturdy boy, as big as his mother, not as tall as Leif, his older brother, but already heavier. Sigurd was the family expert with bow and arrow, best of all the boys in the village, and a fine hunter. He never left home without his bow and arrows, even on wood-gathering trips.

Sigurd's father had been ill for two years and bedridden since midwinter. He had hoped to recover as the weather improved, but his cough was worse now than a month ago, and he was weaker. Sigurd feared the outcome, and every morning as he gathered wood he spoke prayers to the forest spirits for his father's recovery.

After the prayers, he sat quietly in the stillness.

Raising his head at a distant noise, he was startled to see a plume of dark smoke above the hidden western part of the village. He jumped anxiously to his feet, shouldered his load of firewood, and started downstream toward home, hurrying as much as possible considering the weight of wood on his back. The path dropped steeply, and he soon lost sight of the village. He passed through the lower forest at a trot and had nearly reached the fields upstream from the village when he heard screaming. He rushed forward to where he could see what was happening.

The village was in flames. Gangs of armed warriors ran from house to house setting fires and killing any who emerged. Every house was burning, the flames roaring, merging above the village into a tower of black smoke.

Sigurd knew his family was dead or dying. His father, brother, sister. His mother.

He saw at least fifty attackers, more than enough to overwhelm the village even if there had been warning. The screams of women mixed with battle shouts as men sought to defend themselves, but they were too few and were struck down, every one.

Sigurd could not possibly change the outcome.

The scene felt unreal to him, and he stood numb. Fifty armed men had burned a village and killed nearly a hundred people too fast for him to comprehend, his conscious self crushed between the enormity of the act and its impossible quickness.

"SIGURD!"

He turned to see a younger village boy looking dumbly at the slaughter.

"Gunnar." The sound of Sigurd's own voice surprised him; he had thought he would never speak again. "You don't have your bow and arrows?"

"We should hide. Or they'll kill us too."

"They won't come here. They came down the river from the west. I first saw fire from the upper forest. It was behind the western hill. They'll continue downriver toward the sea." Already the attackers were gathering downstream from the village, herding dozens of goats, sheep, and pigs, the village's chief wealth. The boys could see the men and animals clearly.

Gunnar stood sobbing. A cold rain spattered about the two boys. Sigurd felt a sick despair but knew that yielding to it would change nothing, that in the time it usually took him to eat breakfast, the world had turned completely around to face into darkness and horror. He knew in his bones that he would need all his wits and energy simply to stay alive. Grief would have to wait.

SIGURD HAD HEARD ALL HIS LIFE of the Raiders from the North, who ransacked and burned and killed without mercy, but those stories were old ones. He remembered both his grandmothers, who told terrible tales from their youth, although always finishing with how the raiders had been beaten back and thirty peaceful years had passed. His grandparents feared raiders would return. His mother and father hoped otherwise.

Sigurd and Gunnar spent the rest of the day and all that night huddled in the forest, in the rain, without fire or food. The marauders camped downstream from the village with a huge bonfire and in the morning walked off eastward toward the sea. The boys entered the village then—together, so that neither would face alone what they knew they would find.

The rain had stopped, but the day was much colder. Everything was soaked, and the village smelled of sodden ashes and death. Bodies lay everywhere, most of them badly burned. Houses with thatch roofs burn quickly as flaming pieces of the roof fall in; most of the houses were reduced to ash. Of Gunnar's house the boys found only remnants, and in the ash and burned rubble they found no trace of Gunnar's family. At Sigurd's house the posts were still standing. The charred body of Sigurd's father lay where his bed had been. Sigurd found a small body outside the house; turning it over, he recognized his sister. He searched the area for his mother and brother, but to no avail.

He carried his sister to the forest, where the boys had spent the night, and then returned for his father. On that trip he found a stone shovel blade and carried it back to dig a grave. He laid the two bodies side by side and covered them. Gunnar helped with the digging and sobbed quietly as Sigurd spoke the prayers for the dead.

"I WISH I HAD DIED TOO," Gunnar said. He and Sigurd sat at their fire. It was nearly dark. They had set out hunting in the early afternoon, but when he realized Gunnar was a liability, Sigurd asked him to build and tend a fire instead. The hunt dragged on all afternoon, and Sigurd was lucky to return with a poor thin winter rabbit. Gunnar had made a foraging trip to the village by himself and returned with fire tools, a knife blade from which the handle had burned away, and an undamaged bone-handled flint hunting knife.

The boys ate every morsel of rabbit, their only food in two days.

"Do not speak those wishes," Sigurd said. "Do not think them. We were chosen to live, and we must abide by that." Even as he said the words he knew their falseness, that given the choice, he too would rather have died than face life without his family. That night as he lay awake trying to come to terms with his loss, he planned the following morning's hunt and wondered whether he was strong enough and skilled enough to live on his own, especially providing for a younger boy.

LIFE IS SIMPLE at the level of the essentials. Find a way to stay warm—or die of cold. Find food—or starve. The nights were cruel even in good weather, and that spring was a time of unrelenting cold rain. Sigurd dreamed of killing a deer some early morning or late evening, but the does were wary and the bucks scarce, and he was lucky to take enough rabbits to survive.

Sigurd and Gunnar hiked upstream, heading for a smaller village several days' walk away in a different watershed, over a mountain pass. Sigurd was unwilling to share the flat river plain with the raiders. It grew colder as the boys climbed, and by the third day their path was covered with snow. Their hide shoes soaked through, and they camped under an overhanging rock face, where Sigurd built a fire to dry them out.

They were finally dry by the time they slept that night, but they awoke to shrieking wind and long before morning were in the midst of a spring blizzard.

"This can't last long, at this time of year," Sigurd said.

Gunnar did not respond. He was a slighter child than Sigurd and cold through. Their overhanging rock protected them from much of the wind and snow, but when Sigurd tried to rekindle the fire, the wind defeated him. The two boys huddled together for warmth and did not sleep the rest of the night.

BY FIRST LIGHT the storm slackened to occasional flurries, but the snow on the ground was deeper than the day before. Heavy overcast hid the sun, and the day was icy cold. As Sigurd built a fire and prepared to set out hunting, he was anxious about Gunnar, who was lethargic and pale after going without food for a full day.

They had camped well above the stream and the river of cold air that follows it. Sigurd approached the stream cautiously to avoid spooking any game there and saw the doe at the moment she sensed him. She whipped her head toward him, ears up, looking for motion. Sigurd froze. By the time the doe convinced herself that she was not threatened and resumed browsing, Sigurd was numb with cold, barely able to move. He decided to try a difficult shot rather than risk scaring the deer away by going closer. He edged silently behind a tree and pumped his arms to dispel the numbness in his hands. Still out of the deer's sight, he notched an arrow and drew the bow. Then, ever so slowly, he stepped out from behind the tree.

The doe was looking intently downstream. She exploded into motion as a screaming child ran into view with two wolves in grim pursuit, closing fast. Sigurd turned toward the boy, who was stumbling in panic. Sigurd guessed he was about six.

"Over here!"

As the boy looked up, the lead wolf sprang. Sigurd's arrow struck him in the chest, and he crumpled in mid-leap. Sigurd notched another arrow and turned to face the second wolf, but the pursuit was over. The boy leapt behind Sigurd, and the second wolf veered off and ran. The fallen wolf lay still, dying.

"Are you hurt?"

The boy shook his head.

"Are you alone?"

Another shake of the head. "My mother . . . I was ahead, and the wolves chased me. I thought they would catch me."

"Your mother is here?"

The boy pointed back along the path. As Sigurd looked that way, a woman appeared, panting as she ran up the stream with her heavy pack.

The boy ran to her. "Mama, the wolves wanted to kill me, but he shot one and saved me."

The mother's relief came out as an angry outburst. "Ragni, I *told* you to stay close. Don't you *ever—*"

She broke off and looked at Sigurd. "You're only a boy yourself. What are you *doing* here?"

Sigurd drew a deep breath and told the story in a rush. "I am Sigurd, and I'm not only a boy. I'll be fourteen at midsummer. I came from Elvdal with a younger boy after a raid four days ago. The raiders killed everyone in Elvdal and then went toward the river. We are trying to reach Fjellheim. My friend is cold and hungry and maybe sick. I was hunting when I saw your son and the wolves."

The woman looked silently at Sigurd and then put her hand on his arm. "I spoke hastily, Sigurd, and I am sorry. You saved my son. Thank you." She looked into Sigurd's eyes. "I am Asah, and this is Ragnar. We are going home to Fjellheim. I came to Elvdal with my husband to get Ragnar. He had spent the winter there with my husband's parents. The day before the raid, Ragnar took me downstream to see the waterfall, which he loved, and we camped there. We saw the fires and the raiders as we returned in the morning. We hid until they went east. We wept as we walked through the village. Then we started home."

She paused and then said quietly, "My husband and his parents were in Elvdal when the raiders came. We searched but did not find them."

"My mother and father and brother and sister were there," Sigurd said. "I was out gathering wood. So was my friend." He looked at her pack. "Do you have food? I am afraid for him. He is cold and weak."

"I have food, and I will try to help your friend. Then you will both come with me to Fjellheim and stay with my family."

"Thank you for your kindness. If you don't have enough food for that journey, we could cook and eat the wolf."

"I would rather eat the straps of my pack. I have plenty of food."

Sigurd stooped over the body of the wolf and retrieved his arrow. Then he led Asah and the boy Ragnar toward the camp where Gunnar waited.

SIGURD HAD NOT KNOWN Gunnar well. Gunnar was four years younger, the same age as Sigurd's younger brother Kani. Gunnar and Kani had often played together when they were small—their mothers had been friends as children. But Kani sickened and died at age six, and after that Sigurd saw Gunnar only occasionally.

Gunnar was small for nine, and Sigurd's concern for him was well founded. Gunnar had lost his family and had seen too much horror and gone too long without warmth or food. Sigurd saw him curled quiet and pale on the ground and feared he might have died. Gunnar did respond, if barely, when Sigurd shook his shoulder, but then lapsed back into sleep, or near-sleep, and Sigurd could not rouse him.

Asah knelt by the boy, her face near his. Then she straightened up. "Sigurd, I think he's simply hungry and cold. Can you build a fire?"

The ground was clear of snow underneath the overhanging rock. Once the fire flared to life, Gunnar stirred toward it. Asah opened her pack, and Sigurd saw that it contained many dried plants. Asah took a small pot from her pack, filled it with water and crushed a leaf into it, and put it near the fire. While it heated, she crushed a different leaf, rubbing her hands together, and then stroked Gunnar's face and head. Gunnar's eyes opened, and he looked from Sigurd to Asah in apparent confusion. Asah reached beneath him, lifted him a little, and brought the pot of warm liquid to his mouth. "Drink this."

Gunnar drank, sighed, and lay back. "I thought I was dying, but now I'm hungry. We didn't eat at all yesterday."

"Your spirit is suffering from the loss of your family," Asah said, "and your body from cold and hunger, but you are a strong boy, and once you have had enough to eat you will feel better." She reached into her pack. "I have venison for a few days for all of us."

By noon the sun broke through the clouds, and the day began to warm. The woman and the three boys rested and ate, and the companionship they provided each other soothed their grief. "If the weather clears," Asah said, "we could be in Fjellheim tomorrow. With snow on the ground it would take two or three days, but I suspect tomorrow will be warm and dry."

Child of Fire

THE TWO VOICES blend in the hypnotic rhythms of a song of prayer. The women look alike, with dark curly hair and dark eyes. They face a fire; behind them stands a throng of people of all ages. The cool clear midnight twilight is brightened by the full moon.

When the prayer concludes, the two stand silently facing the moon. After a time, they turn to the group. The younger woman leaves her mother to join a blond man and three small children. The crowd sits.

The older woman walks slowly, but her voice is strong and clear. "Overhead is the full moon of midsummer, and we gather to remember our history and speak of the future." Two men thump a hollow log in a repetitive rhythm. The sound is quiet and muffled, eerie in the night, and young children cling to their mothers.

"Forty-seven winters ago they came to the Benchland, our four founders—Zoan and Quitana, my parents, and Sigurd and Inge, parents of Kyle, Alys's husband. They were drawn here by the spirit of this place, the spirit that sustains us. We live in its embrace. It protects us and comforts us and shows us the way

forward." She stands with eyes closed, her body swaying slightly, and her speech falls naturally into the rhythm of the log drum. She has heard these ceremonies all her life. In recent years, she has been the speaker. She is Ana, the group's spiritual leader, its woman of wisdom.

"I loved them, all four. I heard them speak at the festival of the midsummer moon, and as a child I sat on their laps and heard their stories. Now they are gone, and it falls to me to speak for them." Something in her voice catches everyone's attention. A pulse of anticipation ripples through the crowd, almost fear. The drumbeat quickens.

"We have lived here in peace all that time, because our founders fought for us, but largely because our Benchland is beyond the reach of enemies. Now some of us live off the Benchland in houses near the river. Uncle Sigurd disapproved, because he came to manhood in a time of barbarian raids and thought our village below too exposed.

"We owe much to Uncle Sigurd. We live here because he wanted to have a secure place for us to grow. He never changed that view. Preparing for this evening, seeking guidance in the spirit chamber, I dreamed of the last thing he said to me. It is those words I must pass on to you.

"They will return, and the time is not far off. You must prepare to defend the houses near the river."

1

TRIP JOURNAL, Sunday July 1, 12:24 AM—I know all about clustering: nothing ever happens in isolation. Even so, I'm having trouble coming to terms with what happened today.

I'm camping in my truck after spending the day preparing for a one-day cave shoot tomorrow. I was in and out of the cave many times, setting up cameras and flash units and making test shots. I checked email every time I was outside, and I took part in two separate email exchanges from different parts of the world—on the same subject. What's *that* about?

It's past midnight, and I have to be ready at seven when the caving party arrives, but with today's emails on my mind, I can't sleep.

From: kramnick@johnshopkins.edu
To: jarrett@erikssonphoto.com
Date: Sat Jun 30 10:11 AM EDT
Subj: Alice's Cave

> Jarrett - hi from me & Roger. We need to talk,
> said the girl. I've been working again on your
> photos of the tablet paintings from Alice's Cave.
> Weird results are making me nuts. Too complex
> for email. Do you have Skype?

From: jarrett@erikssonphoto.com
To: kramnick@johnshopkins.edu
Date: Sat Jun 30 10:45 AM EDT
Subj: Re: Alice's Cave

> Hi, Mira—Sorry, no Skype. I'm in New
> Hampshire on a job, have phone & iPad, but
> terrible signal. Home tomorrow night. Try me by
> email, so I don't die of curiosity overnight. .../J

From: kramnick@johnshopkins.edu
To: jarrett@erikssonphoto.com
Date: Sat Jun 30 10:49 AM EDT
Subj: Re: Alice's Cave

> You remember the upper entrance? Roger says
> you and he didn't go there but saw it on the
> cave map painted on the wall in the living
> chamber. I've been working with a three-panel
> tablet. Top left, head of a woman, Alice's
> mother. Top right, an overview map showing
> the upper entrance. I really didn't know what the
> tablet showed before now, because the paint
> had crazed, and until I figured out a way to see
> through the crazing, I saw only a scratch maze.

The bottom half of the tablet is a sketch of the upper entrance. And of ME. The drawing is quite clear. I'm wearing caving gear. What could THAT mean? I've never BEEN to the upper entrance.

Call us on Skype when you get home. There's more.

From: jarrett@erikssonphoto.com
To: kramnick@johnshopkins.edu
Date: Sat Jun 30 11:45 AM EDT
Subj: Re: Alice's Cave

I knew about the upper entrance. Re picture of you: Are you sure?

Call you late tomorrow night. ...

MIRA'S EMAILS throw my mind out of sync by five thousand years. Alice's Cave is in Sweden. It's amazing—a big beautiful cave accessible only from an isolated shelf of land that itself is very hard to reach. The paintings Mira mentioned were made there during the Copper Age.

Alice's Cave was the focus of the longest cave expedition of my career. I spent three months there with Mira and Roger, her husband, both scientists as well as expert cavers. She's an anthropologist specializing in prehistoric human cultures, and the samples and photographs we brought back from Alice's Cave have served her well. She returns to studying them whenever her busy schedule permits, and she says she continues to be amazed by the flow of fresh findings from our expedition.

I thought I had put Alice's Cave behind me. I don't dream of it as often as I once did. My experiences there made me question my sanity, and I'm not sure I want to stir those demons again. Perhaps Mira and Roger will have to figure out this new mystery without me.

THE EXCHANGE WITH MIRA is the first part of today's story. Here's the second:

> **From: engberg@stockholmonline.net**
> **To: jarrett@erikssonphoto.com**
> **Date: Sat Jun 30 1:18 PM EDT**
> **Subj: Alice's Cave**
>
> > Mr. Eriksson - I'm Alys Engberg. We met five years ago when you kindly agreed to lead a tour through Alice's Cave. I was then Sweden's Minister of Culture. We laughed together because we had beat-up old caving helmets and the rest of our group looked as clean as Christmas morning.
> >
> > Disturbing things have happened to me recently in Alice's Cave. I'm writing for moral support. Perhaps I'm hoping you can reassure me that I'm not losing my mind. Are you available by phone?
> >
> > Regards - Alys

From: jarrett@erikssonphoto.com
To: engberg@stockholmonline.net
Date: Sat Jun 30 3:01 PM EDT
Subj: Re: Alice's Cave

Alys!! Of course I remember you. I'm on a cave shoot and won't be back in the land of phones until late tomorrow night. Can I call you Monday?

Whatever strange things happened to you in Alice's Cave, I can assure you that stranger ones happened to me, and that if you are losing your mind, I am too. It is a place of spirit power, and it wields a club over my mind.

I can't wait. Tell me what happened. When is a good time to call?

Jarrett

From: engberg@stockholmonline.net
To: jarrett@erikssonphoto.com
Date: Sat Jun 30 3:18 PM EDT
Subj: Re: Alice's Cave

Jarrett - Your email relieves my mind. I'll give you the outline now. I'll be in the air Monday. But for the rest of the week I'll be in the US, in DC. Can we possibly meet? I am committed Tuesday and Thursday, but Wednesday and Friday are free. I'm booked to return Saturday, but if you're not available this week, I'll rebook and meet you later at your convenience.

Alice's Cave is not much visited now. The current Minister feels we did everything necessary to protect it and sees no need for more. I fear he's not interested.

This is not true for me. Alice's Cave has come to dominate my thoughts. Your book usually lies open on my coffee table, and I have dreamed of the spirit chamber many times. I visited the cave alone a few times when I still had legitimate access.

Did you know of the upper entrance? I found it on the remarkable cave map in the living chamber and later spotted the entrance itself from outside. I would never have recognized it as an entrance if I didn't know; from below it appears to be nothing more than a big crack in the cliff. It can't be seen from most of the shelf, because it is behind a ledge. From mountaintop to ledge is a sheer drop, and from the ledge down to the shelf is another. The bottom line is I have recently made two more visits to the cave, rappelling down to the upper entrance. Something other-worldly happened to me. I want to go there with you, if you're willing.

I probably should not discuss any of this by email.

Alys

From: jarrett@erikssonphoto.com
To: engberg@stockholmonline.net
Date: Sat Jun 30 4:55 PM EDT
Subj: Re: Alice's Cave

Alys, nothing about Alice's Cave surprises me. I am ready to believe anything. Since you'll be in

DC, I can make my point clearly if you'll let me show you a cave artifact I keep in my living room. I doubt you'll spend any more time concerned about your sanity. I live in Baltimore. It's a short train ride from DC, and I'll pick you up. Wednesday is perfect—it's a US holiday.

Yes, I will go to Alice's Cave with you.

I'll see you Wednesday. Call me when you have a moment, and we'll set it up. Or email. Or Skype.

Jarrett

SUNDAY JULY 1, 11:12 PM—I'm not far from home, thank God. I'm dictating this to my phone as I drive. I'll transcribe it into the journal tomorrow.

Today was awful. I didn't get to sleep until after two this morning. My dreams were all about Alice's Cave, of course, and I've thought about yesterday's emails all through this long day.

Under glass in my living room is a clay tablet from Alice's Cave with an ancient painting of me, so it is plausible that Mira found a picture of herself. There's only one problem: Mira says it shows her at the cave's upper entrance, which none of us visited.

Alys Engberg, whom I'll meet next Wednesday, was an activist as Minister of Culture. She spearheaded the project to restore the cave entrance after a huge landslide. I last saw her five years ago in Alice's Cave, at the ceremony marking the completion of the restoration.

Enough. I'm nearly home. I'm too tired to call Mira tonight. That will have to wait. But could someone please explain to me how all this happened on the same day?

2

I SLEEP LATE and pay for it with a vivid and nerve-wracking dream, the third cave dream in three nights.

> *The spirit chamber! I have been here so often that it seems like home, but I am always aware that the spirit could crush me like a bug. I woke up here two hours ago and have been waiting for something to happen. The cave is chilly—below sixty—and I am not dressed for it. I'm concerned that I might not be able to get out. Where is Alys? She told me she would meet me here.*

Is the cave moving back into the foreground of my life? After our summer expedition, I had cave dreams every night until the book was published. They are less frequent now, but I will probably have dreams of Alice's Cave forever.

I finish my coffee and have begun unpacking when Mira calls on Skype. Roger is with her.

"Did you get home OK? Can you talk now?" Mira sounds tense.

"Sure. I was in bed before midnight and slept most of twelve hours. I dreamed of the spirit chamber. How are you guys doing?"

"I'm having another attack of cave insanity. I've been working for weeks on the program I told you about. It's finally running, and I'm drowning in new information."

Mira and Roger came to dinner three months ago, and I heard a great deal about her idea for postprocessing images of paintings. Some tablets are partially obscured by crazing. Mira's program clears that up somehow. She explained it in her usual way—in rapid-fire Polish English, becoming less and less comprehensible as she got excited.

"At the micro level, the crazing follows jagged patterns that are almost regular—like lightning. Very different from painted lines. When I remove the crazing, it leaves fine detail I've never seen before. Such as me in the upper entrance, on the tablet I used for testing."

"Can you send me that image?"

"Sure." She turns away from Skype briefly. When her email arrives, I have to agree with her—without question, the ancient image shows Mira in modern caving gear.

Mira comes back to Skype. "Each image takes a great deal of my time. I hope to improve the program, but right now the process is slow—days for each one. Even so, I have many new images, and that's not all. Do you remember the time I found myself actually in the scene? I'm sure you haven't forgotten how I flipped out."

"The battle."

"Yesterday I was staring at a tablet painting and slipped into it. Only briefly, but I knew immediately what was happening. I was in the spirit chamber, upstream from the pool. People were holding a ceremony. They had a fire. I could hear them singing. I freaked."

"You don't *sound* freaked."

"You haven't been here," Roger says quietly. "It's déjà vu all over again."

"Now what, Mira? Will you press on?"

"I don't know. To start with, I'm talking to you."

"You don't know the whole story. I've been exchanging email with Alys Engberg, the Culture Minister you met."

"Oh. Her."

I recall that Mira said Alys drove her nuts with questions during the project to reopen the entrance.

"She wants to talk about the cave too. She'll be in DC next week, and we're going to meet."

"Jarrett, I have to get back into the cave. There are things about it we haven't figured out, but that's only the anthropology part of the reason. The cave is pulling on me."

"Me too. I'll call you after I hear from Alys. Maybe we should go together."

Roger's head is in his hands. "Are we ready for this?"

AFTER THE CALL, I finish unpacking my gear and spend the rest of a long day working on the pictures from the shoot. I'll finish them tomorrow.

In the evening I exchange more email with Alys Engberg.

From: engberg@stockholmonline.net
To:　jarrett@erikssonphoto.com
Date:　Mon Jul 2 8:22 PM EDT
Subj:　Alice's Cave
I'm in DC, exhausted. I'll be through tomorrow at four. Are you available for dinner?

Child of Fire

From: jarrett@erikssonphoto.com
To: engberg@stockholmonline.net
Date: Mon Jul 2 8:29 PM EDT
Subj: Re: Alice's Cave

Alys - The 5:17 train from DC arrives in
Baltimore at six. I'll pick you up. I'm eager to
hear about your cave experiences.

See you tomorrow!

I HAVEN'T SEEN ALYS ENGBERG since we met five years ago in Alice's Cave. She wore a caving helmet that day, but in the train station I recognize her immediately. She is an unusual admixture of ethnic types—her face is Nordic in shape but not coloring, with dark hair and eyes. I spent six months preparing the photographs for the book, including many of Alice's self-portraits, and when I met Alys in the cave she seemed like Alice in modern dress.

We go to a fine restaurant in Baltimore, a place I bring prospective clients. We eat well, with a spectacular city view from the table. Alys says she'd rather not discuss her cave experiences in public, so over dinner we talk about other things, including cave photography and the craziness of DC. She's bright and a good conversationalist.

The drive home takes only a few minutes, and on the way I open the discussion of the cave. "Let's begin with my story. I'll confess in advance that the ancient cave artifact in my living room explains everything."

She raises her eyebrows.

I TURN ON THE DISPLAY LIGHTING as we walk into the apartment. "Welcome to Alice's Cave. While you look around and gasp, can I get you a glass of wine?"

I have practiced this theatrical gesture on many visitors.

The walls of my living room are all but papered in photographs from the book, more than a hundred large glossies, extending into the dining room. I spent weeks on the lighting, which is perfect, if I may say so. The ambient light is low; only the photos are fully lit. Bench seats face the wall to make it easier to view the lower photos.

Many of the pictures are of Alice's paintings, showing the people she lived with and the cave as it looked then. Self-portraits show her at various ages. The display also includes my photos of the cave as it is today—the shelf outside, the entrance, the living chamber. And the spirit chamber. Its reflecting pool and glistening columns look the same in Alice's paintings and my photographs, but neither conveys the impact of the place. Only dreams do that. The feeling is too intense to be simply remembered.

My gallery conveys the idea of the cave in a way that always moves me. I can see it moves Alys too. She walks slowly around the room. "This is overwhelming. I miss the sound of the stream. Otherwise I feel I'm there." She is exactly right. I've often thought I should have recorded the sound of the stream. It's a big part of the cave experience, and in my apartment I always notice its absence.

I circle the room with her, lost once again in the images of the cave. When we complete the tour, I bring up the light in the glass display case in the center of the room, with its two paintings of me on an ancient clay tablet.

A moment passes before Alys understands. "Oh! My God. This is *you*." Next to the tablet is Mira's certificate saying the paint was carbon dated to five thousand years.

Alys sinks onto a bench seat and stares up at the tablet.

"This is Alice, the artist. I met her when she was about eleven." I bring up the light on the best of Alice's adult self-portraits, near the display case. She is perhaps twenty, reflected in the spirit chamber's pool. A torch lights her face, and Alys surely sees how much it resembles her own.

Long pause, with an incredulous look.

"You met her?"

"We saw each other."

"So it's not just me. Please tell me the story of these paintings of you."

MY MARRIAGE ENDED not long before Alice's Cave entered my life, and since then I've been free of the distractions women provide. My apartment is a showcase for my pictures of the cave, a museum of which I am director and curator. It is not designed to bring women into my life. But Alys reacts to the cave exactly as I do, and our shared sense of awe leaves me uncomfortable. What is it I fear? A cliff, at the bottom of which lie the jagged rocks of relationship? Acknowledging the essential loneliness of my life?

"Jarrett," Jeannie said as she left, "you need to live alone with your cameras and pictures and your caving. I'm through standing between you and your destiny." Single is both good and bad. Nights alone are balanced by spur-of-the-moment caving trips without explanation or defense. I have often thought of Alys Engberg. From our first meeting I've had the illogical feeling that we've known each other for years. Thousands of years. But Jeannie was right, and in any event I am too busy to make room for a woman in my life.

As I relate the story of the eleven-year-old artist who painted my picture and kept it safe for all that time, I suspect Alys also senses a potential entanglement between us. Does she share my apprehension?

The authors

JAY HOSLER AND PEGGY HARRISON are professional musicians, chamber music colleagues for more than forty years. They began writing fiction collaboratively in 2011 and have numerous works in progress. They have published the first two volumes of *Norm and Burny*, a five-book series for middle readers, and the three-volume *Benchland* series. *Spirit Chamber* is the second volume.

Peggy Harrison lives in Keller, Texas, with her husband, Paul; Jay Hosler lives in Santa Cruz, California with his wife, Mary.

Praise for *Rockslide*

. . . a delight to read. Better than a movie, and exactly the experience a book is meant to give. Thank you for the escape to another beautiful place and time. Can't wait for The Spirit Chamber.

. . . a book I would love to have read aloud to my fifth graders . . . I was always on the lookout for books that modeled strong, affirmative relationships among people. The cave people genuinely cared for one another and respected their diverse characters and abilities. It is good to see the women presented as strong, resourceful, and intelligent . . . pulse-racing danger. Even at my age, I was completely caught up in it.

. . . The reader is likely to be captivated by this story of the sheer will of several people thrown together by fate . . . Don't be surprised if this story tugs at the soul.

Reviews from amazon.com

Praise for *Norm and Burny*

"I wouldn't hesitate to recommend for advanced readers of seven and up as long as they're in good company to keep from getting too scared. By age nine, they shouldn't need to hide under the bed . . . Highly recommended."

"Good humor, exciting adventures, charming characters, and lovely illustrations."

"I curled up in bed with crackers and milk and had 2 1/2 glorious hours of regression to my childhood."

"If you love animals or have ever tried to imagine what they might be thinking, you will find this to be a quite wonderful tale . . . The Illustrations were beautiful. This book is funny & heart warming with characters you'll love . . . especially the dog."

"We just finished reading this book as one of our home school read-aloud selections. It was a Christmas gift. My daughter (11) says it is now one of her favorites. My son (9) thought it was good. We can't wait for the second book."

"The sophistication and humor are well balanced with the excitement of the adventures."

Reviews from amazon.com

If you enjoyed this book . . .

Please write a review

Your review on **amazon.com** and **goodreads.com**
will help promote the book!

Please visit Benchland.org

Buy our books!
Join our mailing list—be the first to know!
Keep in touch by liking our Facebook page.

Watch for Book Three of the *Benchland* series

Tell your friends about *Spirit Chamber!*

www.ingramcontent.com/pod-product-compliance
Lightning Source LLC
Chambersburg PA
CBHW020739250626
47155CB00003B/830